PRAIRIE DOG TOWN

by
Janette Oke

Illustrated by Brenda Mann

Other Janette Oke
Children's Books in this Series:

Spunky's Diary
New Kid In Town
The Prodigal Cat
Ducktails
The Impatient Turtle
A Cote of Many Colors
Maury Had a Little Lamb
Trouble in Fur Coat
This Little Pig
Pordy's Prickly Problem
Who's New at the Zoo?

A Prairie Dog Town
Copyright © 1988
Janette Oke
All Rights Reserved

Published by Bethany House Publishers
A Ministry of Bethany Fellowhship International
11400 Hampshire Avenue South
Minneapolis, Minnesota 55438
www.bethanyhouse.com

Cover Illustration by
Brenda Mann

Printed in the United States of America

ISBN 0-934998-31-0

To Jessica Brianne Logan
who was born on January 16, 1988
to Marvin & Laurel,
little sister of Nathanael.
Your Grandpa and Grandma Oke
welcome you with love and thanksgiving.

DONATED

IN MEMORY

OF
BABY SISTER
SHARON ANN SMITH
BY
PAT SMITH

Table of Contents

Chapter One

Introductions

I rolled my eyes heavenward and sighed deeply. How would I ever remember all of the things that Mother was saying? She had already been talking for what seemed like hours, and we, her offspring, were to know, backward and forward, all of the instructions that she was giving us. *We'd* never remember. *I'd* never remember. There was just too, too, much. Besides, it was most difficult to concentrate. All that I could really think about was my eagerness to enter the exciting world above ground. I hadn't even been allowed a peek yet but I knew from the conversation of my mother and father that there were things to see that I couldn't even imagine.

"And remember!" Mother was saying, "If ever you hear the signal, stop whatever you are doing and remain perfectly still. Don't even whisk your tail or blink your eye. If the signal comes the second time, then dash for home without even waiting to determine why. Just run. Do you hear me? Run!"

There was a small stirring beside me and I couldn't resist turning my head ever so slightly. Mother had sternly admonished us that all eyes were to be held steadily on her as she spoke. I dared not disobey her.

Out of the corner of my eye I saw Frisk, my brother, roll his eyes and shake his tiny head much as I had just done. Without shifting my gaze totally from Mother, I was able to give Frisk just the tiniest wink. He caught it. I heard him fighting to hide a snicker.

"What if we don't hear a second signal?" someone was asking.

It was Annabelle. She *would* ask questions and delay our getting out. In my thinking, she was Mother's pet. She always sat and listened and asked questions and made the rest of us look bad.

"If there is not a second signal to follow the first, then you may go right on eating," Mother responded, just as though eating would be the only thing that we would busy ourselves with once we were out.

"How long should we wait?" asked Annabelle, and I secretly wished that I was close enough to nip her.

"Count slowly to ten," said Mother. "If you are still unsure, count again."

"Do we go right down to our nest?" Annabelle asked again.

"No," answered Mother. "You may stop at a 'listening' room near the entrance. If you hear any further noise, then you quickly run to the nest. If you wait for some time and nothing further happens, you may carefully resurface. But remember, do it cautiously."

Annabelle nodded solemnly. I was afraid that she was going to come up with yet another question but Mother changed the format.

"Now let's review," she said. "What are we to watch for?"

Oh, boy! I thought of a couple dozen things right off that I wanted to watch for, but Annabelle was dutifully spielling forth.

"Shadows—that might mean a hawk in the sky. Movement—that might mean a coyote or fox or bobcat out hunting. Snakes."

Mother beamed at Annabelle. "You've listened very well, my dear," she said.

Annabelle squirmed her pleasure and glanced sideways at our sister Louisa. Then she just couldn't refrain from turning to give Frisk and me a smug look.

"And what can we eat?" asked Mother.

Annabelle started to answer but Frisk cut in. I think he did it just so Annabelle couldn't.

"There are a number of roots and grasses," he said. "We just need to watch the adults to know which ones are best."

"Good, Frisk," said Mother, but she didn't beam at him like she had at Annabelle.

I hoped that she was finally going to let us go but she didn't. She went right on.

"Remember, our town is a nice safe place to live, with many friends and neighbors. Everything that you need is right here. There is no reason for you to be unhappy. But you must remember the rules of good relationships. All of the town is divided into territories or coteries. No one trespasses on our territory and we do not trespass on the territory of another. That is the only way to live peaceably with the neighbors. Is that clear?"

We all nodded dutifully.

"Your father and I are very strict about the rules," went on Mother. "We don't ever want to hear a report that our children are careless about following them."

"No, Mother," we said in unison.

I thought that we were never going to be able to escape Mother's lecturing and get a look at the big world that I understood was waiting for us just outside the entrance of our home. My tail twitched restlessly and my whole body felt tingly. It was all that I could do to hold myself in check while Mother went on.

"We have a wonderful town, but it isn't without enemies. Your father and I want you to be safe—as well as happy. Observe the rules and you will be both."

Little Sue Mary squirmed. I couldn't see Sue Mary because Mother insisted that we look at her when she was speaking, but I could feel the impatient wiggle brush up against my side.

Sue Mary was the youngest of our litter and the smallest. She was much smaller than Louisa who was content to eat and sleep her way through life. She was also smaller than Annabelle, though Annabelle wasn't content to sleep. She was much too busy pleasing Mother. Sue Mary was also smaller than Frisk and me, who were about the same size, somewhere in between Louisa and Annabelle.

But Sue Mary was my favorite. Oh, I got along alright with the rest of my sisters and I certainly had some good times with Frisk, but it was Sue Mary that shared my deepest secrets and also my

fun. I did hope that when Mother finally lined us up to get our first look at the outside world that I would be stationed next to Sue Mary. That was why I pressed in close beside her now.

"Always—always—when you leave the nest, stop at the entrance before you even put your head out, and listen and sniff. Listen and sniff. Check to see if there are any signs of enemies. Then when you put your head out, always, always, take time to spot the sentries on duty. Locate them and fix them firmly in your mind. You will be much more likely to hear their danger signal if you know exactly where they are stationed."

Sue Mary trembled again and I wasn't sure now if it was fright or excitement that shook her tiny body. I pressed just a bit closer to her. "Now," said Mother, "your father is waiting outside. He has gone out to check carefully to see if it is safe for your first trip up-top."

Now *I* began to tremble, but I knew that my shaking was due to excitement. What would it be like? Would it be as exciting as it sounded when Mother and Father spoke of the outside world? Was it really as big as they said? Was the food really that good? Were there really neighbors with youngsters like us, all around us as far as my eye could see? I trembled again.

"Now let's line up," Mother was saying and little Sue Mary pressed herself close to me as though she feared that Mother might separate us.

"Annabelle, you follow me. Frisk, you follow Annabelle. Then Louisa, Sue Mary, and Flick you bring up the rear."

I began to inwardly protest. Why should I be the very last one to see the outside world? Why should everyone, even Annabelle, get to see what lay beyond our burrow before me? And then I heard Sue Mary let out a little sigh of pleasure and I knew that she was pleased that I would be right behind her and my anger began to cool.

"Remember to think! Think! Think!" said Mother. "As long as you use the mind that the Creator has given to you, you will be just fine in the outside world. Now, let's go. Slowly and carefully. There is no need to be impatient. The world outside will not disappear in the next few minutes. It will still be there for you. So be cautious."

Mother began to slowly, slowly, climb the tunnel that led upward. I had spent most of my young life in the snug nest at the bottom of the tunnel. I had been to the storage rooms that led off the main hall, but that was as far as any of us had been allowed to go. And now we were on our way to the top. All the way to the top. We'd even get to see what lay beyond. I pushed Sue Mary slightly in my impatience, but it didn't hurry anything. Sue Mary was boxed in by those in front of her.

We climbed up and up. I hadn't realized that our tunnel was so long. On and on we went and then suddenly we stopped. My frustration grew, but back down the line of small bodies came the whisper. "Mother is about to leave the burrow. She is listening and sniffing."

My excitement mounted.

We inched forward slightly. Then came the whisper, "Annabelle is listening now." I wished that I was closer so I could give Annabelle the nudge that would send her out into the new world.

It seemed an insufferably long time until we got to inch forward again. Annabelle was taking all of

Mother's admonitions very seriously. She must have listened and sniffed and sniffed and listened and listened and sniffed over and over again. At long last we were able to move forward again.

We stopped while Frisk took his turn checking the safety of the unknown and then we moved on again. Frisk hadn't taken nearly as long as Annabelle. Louisa was next. By the time that she moved carefully into listening position, I could see brightness beyond her, framing her plump body as she hesitated in the doorway.

I could hardly stand it. I wanted to push my two sisters aside and rush out into the newness of the outside world. But I knew that it was forbidden. I knew that I must obey Mother.

Louisa finally emerged and then it was Sue Mary who moved cautiously near the entrance. I could see the brightness spilling all about her smooth, tan coat. She stood trembling and I wondered secretly if she could even listen and sniff in her intense excitement. Then I remembered that Mother and Father were up-top, listening and sniffing on our behalf, and I relaxed. Sue Mary would be quite safe.

Hesitantly she poked her tiny head above ground and I heard the gasp that escaped her. She just sat there, her small head rotating first this way and then that, and she looked and looked and let little sounds of pleasure and excitement gurgle up in her throat.

I knew that she was entranced by the spectacle before her. I also knew that she was blocking my way. I couldn't wait to see what she was seeing. I gave her a small nudge and when there was little response, I pushed her more firmly.

"Oh, Flick," she whispered. "It's beautiful! So big! So—!"

"I'd like to see it for myself," I said rather impatiently, then softened somewhat. "Please. Please!"

She moved aside then. But not far. She just moved over so that I could leave the burrow also and she still sat right there, drinking in the new world and waiting for me.

I could hardly stop to listen and sniff. I was so anxious to see what Sue Mary was enjoying.

I tried. I mean, I really tried. I did stop—sort of. And I did tilt my head to listen, first one way and then the other. And I did take one big long sniff, and then I poked my head out of the entrance and looked at the world beyond our tunnel.

For a minute I saw absolutely nothing. The brightness of the sun completely blinded me. I blinked and blinked, trying to get things to focus properly, and then slowly I could see shapes and movement—and distance. Oh, my, such distance. The world just went on and on and on. I had had no idea that it was so big.

"Isn't it magnificent?" whispered Sue Mary, and I pushed my way out of the entrance to perch on the sandy mound beside her.

"Did you spot the sentries?" came a stern voice to my left and I realized that Mother was right there, watching and waiting as each of her children made their exit from the nest.

I looked around me then. Over to my right was a large prairie dog with sharp black eyes and a stub of a tail. He stood on his hind legs, his eyes darting back and forth over the whole area before him. Now and then he tilted his head and looked toward the sky. As I watched, he shifted his body slightly

so that he could easily scan the area to his right.

"Him?" I asked Mother.

"That's one," Mother replied. "I want you to find at least three of them."

I turned in the other direction. There was another prairie dog on an elevated bit of ground. He was much smaller than the other animal had been. At first I was going to pass right over him, but his bearing stopped me. He was absolutely motionless and silent, but his whole body seemed alert and sensitive to any movement or sound. I watched him for a few minutes. Only his eyes moved.

"Him?" I asked Mother.

She nodded.

"One more."

Sue Mary nudged me and nodded her head just slightly in the direction that lay directly ahead of us. I looked that way and sure enough, standing on a small outcropping of rock was a third sentry. He was a little lighter in color than the other two and he blended in with the rock perfectly. He lowered himself to be lost totally in the color of the rock and then as I watched he lifted himself to his hind legs again and took a thorough look over all of our domain.

"Three," I pointed out to Mother.

She nodded her head and moved forward. "Your father has found a nice patch of grass off this way," she said. "Come, we'll show you what is good eating."

I was a bit impatient with that. I wasn't feeling all that hungry and there was so much to see. I wanted to just look and look. But I knew that I must follow Mother.

Mother must have read my mind for she spoke

softly.

"After you get more familiar with the area and with the rules, you may go off on your own, but for the next few days we want you to stay close to the family."

It bothered me. It seemed that I had been waiting forever and ever to get up-top and see the amazing world. Now here I was with the vast and exciting new world right before me and I had to stay close to Mother.

I choked back my impatience and followed quietly. Exploring would be allowed later; Mother had promised.

Chapter Two

Day One

We joined the rest of the family in a little patch of grass. The morning sun was hot on my back and the sound of the rustling of the grass in the slight wind fascinated me. I could hardly concentrate on eating, though I found that the grass was delicious just as Mother had promised. It was hard to eat and look at the same time.

Mother and Father had been quite right. We did have neighbors, lots of neighbors it seemed. All around us prairie dogs moved about or called to one another.

I would grab a mouthful of the succulent grasses and then lift myself onto my hind legs and stretch my head upward so that I could see all that I could see as I chewed. It was all so fascinating. If I hadn't been so hungry I would have completely forgotten to go back for another mouthful.

Sue Mary fed close beside me. Much like me, she often forgot to eat.

"Look at the colors, Flick," I heard her say and I looked around me. It wasn't the colors that fascinated me. It was the action. But dutifully I scanned the nearby prairie for Sue Mary's colors. There sure were lots of them.

Bright blue and scarlet flowers nodded on short stems as the breeze swept over their heads. Green grass blended into greys and tans and here and there a dark brown added its beauty. Sharp rocks jutted out in soft muted tones of pewter or cream. Overhead the brightness of the morning sun added depth to the blue, blue, of the distant sky where fluffy clouds drifted lazily in a ceaseless game of shape-changing.

Sue Mary was right. There certainly was color.

I grabbed another quick bite and went back to the action.

Just beyond us a family fed together. The children looked about our age and I could see them steal little glances our way every now and then. I longed to go over to make their acquaintance but I knew better than to ask. That was the kind of thing that I would do when Mother gave her permission for us to 'explore.'

Beyond the family two young prairie dogs played a vigorous game of tag. To our left two large members of the community argued over who had first found the patch of tasty roots. Beyond them a single animal fed all alone. Beyond and beyond and beyond, I could see more prairie dogs in various activities. On the rocks nearby two stretched out in the warm sun. Obviously, they had already had their fill of roots and grasses. To their left, another pair reclined. They nudged and cuddled and groomed one another affectionately.

My eyes lifted from the prairie dogs to study who our other neighbors might be. In a nearby cluster of low shrubs a pair of birds fluttered and fussed over a small nest of twigs and feathers. A movement to my right sent the chills through my spine until Mother whispered reassuringly, "It's a jack rabbit. No need for alarm," and she went right on feeding. Overhead, birds flew at intervals and I wondered how in the world I was ever to pick out a hawk among the wings and feathers.

Frisk drew up beside me. He grinned at me and I knew that he had something to share.

"There's another family right over there," he whispered.

"I know," I answered, wondering how he thought that I could have missed them.

"They're watching us," he continued.

"So?" I replied. I didn't say so, but I had been watching them as well. And with his admission, Frisk seemed to have been keeping a close eye on things, too.

"I think they are about our age."

I nodded again, reaching for a quick mouthful so that I could lift myself up again.

"There's only one boy. Three girls and just one boy."

I hadn't noticed that.

"Can you imagine what it would be like to have just sisters?" went on Frisk.

"Depends," I said, casting a sideways glance at Annabelle.

Frisk saw my look and began to snicker.

"Bet he'd sure like some company," Frisk said, trying to sound nonchalant.

"We can't and you know it," I said firmly. "Mother said—."

"I know. I know," said Frisk. "I wasn't saying

'now.' When we can—then I think that we should get to know him."

"Sure," I promised, and went back to eating.

But I didn't have to wait until Mother gave us the okay to get to know our neighbor. I was feeding close to the family when a head poked itself from behind a rock, so close to me that I could have almost touched him. It startled me at first and then I recognized the fella from the nearby family.

"Hi!" he said with a grin.

"Hi," I responded, a bit shyly. I had never met anyone outside of our family before.

"Wanta look around?" he asked.

"Can't. This is our first day out."

"Our first, too," he admitted.

"But our mother and father won't let us leave the family yet," I said and then blushed. It did make us sound terribly immature. "Not today," I quickly added. "As—as soon as we know the area a bit and the—the—rules, then we will be able to look around all we want to."

He just looked at me.

"It's their rules," I said in explanation. "They—."

"My folks have those rules, too," he said with a shrug.

"Then why—?" I began but quickly stopped short. I knew that I shouldn't ask the question.

"We are to be extra careful until—." I began, but he didn't let me finish.

"That's what the sentries are for. Why bother posting them if everyone else has to watch anyway?"

He did have a point.

"They can't see everything," I said lamely but my argument lacked conviction.

I was glad that Frisk was out of earshot. I wasn't sure that it would be wise for him to chat with the young stranger. He was already anxious for a little adventure on his own.

Annabelle moved our way and the new neighbor ducked his head back behind the rock.

Louisa whined. "I'm full."

"Good," said Mother. "And isn't it delicious. Much, much nicer than the dried grasses in the burrow."

Louisa just nodded. Her eyelids looked droopy.

"I'm tired," she said. "I want to go home."

"Very well," said Mother.

I could have nipped Louisa. How could she possibly think of going back to the darkness and blandness of the burrow when one could be up-top drinking in the sunshine and the fresh odor-filled air. Just because of her we would all need to go back into the stuffy nest where nothing ever happened except for an occasional squabble among offspring. But Mother was speaking again.

"You all stay very close to your father. I am taking Louisa back to the nest."

I breathed again and even forgave Louisa.

With a check toward each of the three sentries, Mother left with Louisa closely behind her.

I was full, too. I hadn't wanted to admit it because I was afraid that if I did so I would be ushered back to the safety of the nest. Yet, I didn't see how I would ever hold another bite. I nibbled at a root and didn't bother to chew or swallow.

Father did not seem to be looking my way and so I dared to lift myself up slowly on my hind legs and take a good look around. The young neighbor had rejoined his family. He looked my way and gave me a smug look. I knew that he was telling me that he had sneaked off and returned and no one had even missed him.

I glanced away. And then to my absolute horror I saw something moving directly toward us. It was the biggest moving thing that I had ever seen. It was brownish red in color and long, long sturdy legs lifted and fell to the prairie grasses as it moved. Now and then it snorted a blast of air from somethere beside its devouring mouth. The huge head swung up and down and swept from side to side. The eyes roamed over the grassland, blinking and staring by turn. Behind it a long rope-like thing with a swatch on the end of it swept back and forth, back and forth. I stared in fright and wonder. It was some time before I could find my voice and my legs.

"Father," I cried in a hoarse whisper. "Father, we're being attacked."

Father's head came up quickly and he rose to his hind feet. I saw his glance quickly dart toward the nearest sentry to see if he might have missed a signal.'

My gaze went to the sentry, too. He was there to guard us. He was supposed to be alert, so why hadn't we been warned? What good was a sentry if he just sat there and didn't send the alarm? Or had he already run for cover?

But no. There he sat in perfect calm while the huge animal swung closer and closer toward us. Toward him. He never even flinched.

"Where?" asked Father, and I wondered how in the world he could miss the huge animal.

"Right—right there," I stumbled, shivering at the nearness of the thing.

"That?"

I nodded, trembling until my whole body shook. The monster was almost upon us.

"That's a cow," said Father calmly and he moved aside a few feet to let the huge animal pass by. The whole ground shook with the weight of it. I snuggled against Father and closed my eyes. I was sure that we would be crushed between crunching teeth or smashed beneath huge feet. But nothing happened. After a few minutes the ground ceased to quake and I was still in one piece. I dared to open my eyes. Father was still feeding nearby and the animal had moved off several feet to our right.

"A cow won't hurt you," Father said around his mouthful. "A cow eats grass."

"Oh," I mumbled, trying to sound convinced, but I couldn"t help but add, "but what if they step on you?"

"That would be bad," said Father and I thought that I heard amusement in his voice. "Only, they are big and clumsy and can't move very quickly at all. All we need to do is get out of their way."

"Oh," I said again, but I didn't stop trembling.

Suddenly I felt full and sleepy and—and scared. I was ready to go back and join Louisa in the nest but I sure didn't want to admit to that. Annabelle saved the day for me.

"I'm full," she said, daintily wiping at her mouth. "I think that I'd like to go back to the nest."

Father lifted himself up and looked around him. I could see him carefully taking stock of each of his offspring. He noticed the rounded sides and heavy eyelids.

"It looks like everyone has had enough for one day," he said. "I think it's time that you all went in for a nap."

Then he pulled himself up and checked each of the sentries. There was no sign of impending alarm from any one of them so Father moved forward.

"Come," he said to the four of us and we fell into line behind him.

As we neared home, Mother, who had been feeding near our entrance, joined us and led the way down through the passageway.

Just before I entered the tunnel that would take me down, down, to our waiting nest, I turned and took one more look at the big, outside world. I hated to leave it, but I was so sleepy, and still a little shook up by my experience with the cow-monster. Besides, the world would still be there tomorrow. Mother had promised. I flicked my tail and ducked into our entrance and followed Sue Mary down to the family nest for a much needed nap.

Chapter Three

Louisa

From way back near the end of the line, I heard Mother's sharp gasp.

"What's wrong?" called Father. He had heard her, too.

"Louisa," answered Mother.

"What's the matter with her?" Father began to work his way forward, brushing past those of the family who still stood in the tunnel waiting for Mother to move so that we might enter the nest area.

"She's not here," responded Mother and her voice was tight with emotion.

"Not here? But I thought you—."

Mother didn't even let Father finish.

"I did. I brought her right on home."

By now all of us were worried. We knew, from Mother's lecturing, that we had enemies. Had poor Louisa fallen prey to one of them?

I could sense Father stiffening. His nose began to twitch and I knew that he was checking for any unusual odors.

"It's not a snake. It couldn't be a snake," Mother was saying. "We would have noticed."

"I certainly don't smell—," began Father and Mother cut him off again.

"And I didn't smell anything either."

"Did you stop to check—?"

"I always stop to check." Mother's voice was high-pitched and tense. I knew that she was very near tears. I had never seen her like that before. But then, none of us had ever been missing before.

"Perhaps she slipped back out," said Father.

"She couldn't have," Mother was determined. "I was right there—all the time. I fed not more than ten feet away from the entrance the whole time."

"Did you come down with her when you brought her back?" asked Father and I hoped that Mother wouldn't take the comment as one of reproach. I guess Father thought of that too, for he hurried on. "I just want to gather as much information as I can so that I might try to piece it all together."

Mother hesitated for a moment and I knew that she was fighting to get herself under control. I heard her snuffling back tears that threatened to spill.

"No. No—I—I just brought her to the entrance, checked for anything out-of-the-ordinary, and then—then sent her down."

Father moved closer to Mother. "I'm sure we'll find her," I heard him soothe. He nuzzled his nose against her neck to give her some reassurance. "Why don't you put the children to bed and I'll go take a look around."

Mother nodded and moved forward without speaking but I knew that she was still very worried about Louisa.

We settled down quickly. I guess that we didn't want to give Mother anything more to worry about. I cuddled in between Annabelle and Sue Mary and shut my eyes. I couldn't sleep. I had felt so sleepy and now all I could think about was my sister Louisa. If something happened to her—. But I refused to think about it. I tried to picture the big blue sky, the waving prairie grasses, the sweet roots that I had nibbled on. I even spent some time thinking of the monstrous cow-creature that I had seen. Even that couldn't keep my thoughts from going back to Louisa.

I knew that my sisters and brother were not sleeping either, though no one stirred and no one whispered. Still, I could sense by the tenseness of the bodies curled up beside me that they too were still awake.

The minutes ticked by as hours. All of us waited for the sound of Father returning with our lost sister. But he did not come.

Mother tried to be quiet so we could sleep, but she couldn't. She kept stirring restlessly and I knew that her mind was busy reviewing every move that she made when she brought Louisa home. Had she missed the presence of an enemy? Had she ever turned her back to the entrance while she fed nearby? How could Louisa just disappear? Mother stirred restlessly awaiting Father's quick return.

Frisk was the first one of us to finally manage to fall asleep. Little Sue Mary was next. Annabelle wiggled and squirmed and sniffed and I knew that she was probably more frightened than any of us about Louisa's disappearance. Despite her prissiness, Annabelle did care—for each one of us, I

knew that. I wished there was some way that I
could comfort her but I really didn't know how.

At long last we heard the soft sound of footsteps
on the tunnel floor and we knew that Father was
returning. I raised myself up slightly and strained
to hear or smell if Louisa was with him. He was
alone.

Mother met him at the entrance to the nest and
pushed her nose against his cheek. They talked in
worried whispers and their words easily reached
me where I lay.

"You didn't find her?" This was Mother.

"I looked everywhere."

"Did you ask—?"

"No one has seen her. Not since you brought her
home."

Mother began to sob.

Father ran his nose along her cheek. "Don't cry,
dear," he comforted. "She couldn't just disappear.
She's got to be—."

"But where?" sobbed Mother and she forgot to
hold her voice down. Frisk stirred and Sue Mary
woke up with a start.

"Sh-h-h," said Father, but it was already too late.
The whole nest was roused.

"Are you going out again?" Mother asked Father.

"It's getting dark," Father replied and I could
hear the worry and anguish in his voice.

"But—?" began Mother, and I knew that she was
thinking of Louisa out there in the world of darkness and predators all alone.

"I'll go first thing in the morning," Father promised. "There is nothing more I can do tonight."

Mother began to cry—and then Annabelle joined
her. There was nothing quiet about the way that

Annabelle cried. Mother moved over quickly to comfort her and they cried together. Sue Mary was next and then we were all crying. Father and Mother moved from one to the other of us, comforting and quieting us. It took several minutes before they managed to get some kind of order in the nest. It was Frisk who brought things back to normal—and he wasn't even trying.

"I'm hungry," he said.

A little rumble of surprised gasps ran around our circle and ended up in awkward little chuckles. Father reached over and playfully nuzzled Frisk's left ear.

"I'm sure you are," he said. "It's been several hours since you have eaten. I'll go see what I can find to eat."

Mother sighed and wiped her last burst of tears on a furry paw. It was her resignation that life must somehow carry on.

"The furthest storeroom," she said to Father. "There is still plenty of food there."

Then she turned to us. "Up you get," she said. "Wash up for dinner."

We did. We tumbled out of bed and began to prepare ourselves for the evening meal. I was just starting on my face when I heard a surprised call from Father.

For one awful moment I held my breath. Had he found the enemy? Was there a snake or some other creature in the storage room?

Mother rushed forward. I guess she wondered the same thing for she flung back to those of us in the den, "Don't move. You hear?"

We didn't move.

"What is it?" we heard her call to Father as she

scurried along the passageway.

"Louisa!"

"What?"

"Louisa. She's here."

We all forgot Mother's quick command and pressed forward to see for ourselves. Sure enough, there was Father coming back down the passage with a sleepy Louisa in tow.

Mother rushed forward in a fresh burst of tears and began to greet Louisa so enthusiastically that she nearly upset her. We could see from Louisa's face that she was wondering what all of the fuss was about.

"Where did you find her?" Mother finally asked Father.

"In the first storage room."

"In the storage room?" We could tell that Mother never would have thought to look there.

"What were you doing in the storage room?" she asked Louisa.

Louisa yawned and looked around the room of anxious family members.

"I was sleepy," she shrugged matter-of-factly.

"Couldn't you find your way to your bed?" asked Mother.

Louisa looked puzzled. Then shrugged her shoulders.

"It was too far to the bed," she stated, "so I just went to the storage room."

Mother sighed, a rather exasperated sigh which ended up in a good-natured laugh. "Well, you're home now," she stated. "That's all that matters."

"I was always home," said a bewildered Louisa. She still had no idea of what she had put us all through.

Mother laughed again and let Louisa pass into the den where we all took turns welcoming her. It was so good to have her back. To know that nothing had happened to her. To feel safe again within the confines of our home.

And then our stomachs reminded us again that we really were hungry. Father went back to the task of bringing down some of the dried grasses and roots from the storage area and Mother served us each a portion—giving the largest to Louisa. None of us even complained. We were all so glad to be back together again as a family that we didn't even think about it. In fact Annabelle even slipped a little of her serving to Louisa.

I wouldn't have gone that far. But it sure was good to have Louisa home again.

Chapter Four

Learning

The next morning Mother lined us up again for our trip to the outside world. I was hoping that she would skip the lecture—but she didn't. She went over all of the rules again, very carefully. She even added one more.

"And remember," she said, "if you come back home earlier than the rest, come all of the way down to the nest. Any of the other rooms are too close to the surface and predators."

Mother made no mention of Louisa but we all knew why she added the extra rule.

Then she placed us into the marching line. She revised it somewhat. Louisa followed her, then Sue Mary, then me, then Annabelle and finally Frisk. I was delighted to be so close to the front of the line. That would mean that I would get to see the world much sooner than if I were bringing up the rear.

Again we proceeded slowly. Again, each one had to stop to listen and sniff before leaving the tunnel. Again Father and Mother both supervised us very closely. Still, it was wonderful to be out in the open.

I looked at the wide, blue sky with the lazy clouds.
I sniffed at the fragrance of the prairie wind. I felt
excitement as I watched our many neighbors. It
would have been very easy for me to forget that we
had an enemy in the world.

I guess Father and Mother knew that. They
seemed especially attentive. They fed with the rest
of us but I could see them stop and look and listen
frequently, their heads tilted to the side, their dark
eyes glistening, every nerve alert to any danger
that might be lurking nearby.

I had spotted the closest three sentries when I
left the nest. A big fellow on our right was perched
on a sand hill much above the rest of us. To the left
a smaller, wiry looking younger animal sat on his
haunches jerkily studying this way and that. I saw
Mother look at him anxiously and then I heard her
whisper to Father in a voice that was not meant to
carry to me, "I do hope he knows what he's doing. I
don't trust these young men. I'll bet this is his first
posting."

Father cast an eye in the direction of the sentry.
He kept right on chewing on his bit of sweet grass.

"They have to start sometime," he said.

Then he nodded toward the big fellow. "Notice
who they have posted him with," he went on.
"Fotterby won't let him slip up. He never misses a
thing."

Mother seemed to relax some at Father's words.
She even began to feed again.

The third sentry was on a lookout further upwind
from us. He was lighter in color. I knew that he
was well-seasoned as a sentry. Perhaps too well-
seasoned. He seemed a little too old for the job. I
guess that was why they were training new ones. I

was sure that the older guard should soon retire.

I dismissed the three sentries and began to feast on the prairie grasses. They were so much better than the dry forage that came from our storerooms. I loved the fresh taste. I began to eat hurriedly. Not only was I hungry, but I reasoned that if I could eat my fill quickly, I might have time to do a little looking around before it was time to go back to the nest. I couldn't see myself going home early like Louisa had done. No sirree. If I finished eating before the others, I would use the time to do some exploring. If Mother would let me out of her sight, that is.

Even as I thought about it, I had my doubts. Louisa's little escapade had Mother jittery. I was sure that she wouldn't allow any of us out of her sight for some time to come. I sighed. I was glad that Louisa was safe and sound but I did wish that she hadn't spoiled it for the rest of us.

The bright, morning sunshine suddenly disappeared, making our world seem menacing and shadowed. I stopped my feeding to see what had happened to it. I soon decided that I need not be alarmed for after a brief check, Mother and Father seemed unconcerned and went right on feeding. Still, I couldn't help being a bit worried. I had already learned to love the sunshine.

"What happened?" I asked Frisk, but he just shrugged his shoulders and grabbed another mouthful of grasses.

I decided that he didn't know anymore than I did. I made my way carefully over to Father.

"What happened?" I asked him.

"To what?" He lifted himself up on his hind legs and looked carefully all about us, just to be sure that he hadn't missed something that he should have noticed.

"To the light," I said, puzzled by the lack of it.

"Oh, that," said Father and dropped back down on all fours and began eating again.

"The sun is gone, that's all."

"Where'd it go?" I persisted.

"Just behind the clouds," said Father.

"Will it come back?" I asked, wondering why Father didn't show a little more concern.

"Oh, my yes," laughed Father. "Nothing has ever been able to keep the sun from shining. It might disappear for a while—even a few days at a time—but it always comes back again."

I was relieved to hear that. Still, I did wish that the sun would shine. That was one thing that I liked about being out of doors. Everything looked so bright and sparkling in the sunlight. I liked the feel of the warm rays on my back as well. Now even its warmth was gone.

The wind blew a little brisker, making Father's fur coat shift and split as he fed next to me. I watched in fascination as the air currents shivered across the fur, exposing a seam of the darker, fluffier under-fur as it rippled back and forth.

Mother moved close to us.

"It looks like it might rain," she observed and cast an apprehensive glance at the sky.

"Could," said Father, but he didn't sound worried.

"What's rain?" I asked.

Father smiled. "Rain is water from the sky," he told me.

"Water from the sky?" I couldn't imagine such a thing.

"Like dew," went on Father. "Remember how you got your feet wet when we first came out this morning?"

I nodded slowly. I didn't particularly care for wet feet. I had tried to lift my feet high to avoid the wetness, but of course it hadn't worked.

"Well, rain is like the dew. Only rain comes down from the sky. Sometimes there is a lot of rain all at one time. Everything gets wet."

I made a face. I just knew that I wouldn't like it.

"Oh, we need rain," Father hastened to tell me. "Without it we would soon run out of prairie grasses to eat. The grass needs the rain in order to grow."

I was glad to hear that the rain was good for something. I looked at the sky again. There was no sign of the sun now. Dark-looking clouds moved steadily to the south and the wind shook the nearby grasses and rattled the sagebrush.

"Perhaps we should take them in," I heard Mother say.

I didn't like the wind and should have been glad to line up and return to the nest, but I was curious about rain. What did it look like? How did it feel? I was anxious to discover it for myself. But just as I was sure I was about to find out, Father gave the signal and we quickly fell into line for the trip back to the den. Already Louisa was whimpering in alarm. She didn't like the darkness and she didn't like the wind. Besides, she was already sleepy again and now she was feeling cold. Mother moved to comfort her and then we began to cautiously move toward our home.

We are about halfway there when big spatters of water began to splash all around us. One hit me right on the end of the nose and I ducked and squeaked in surprise. Then another one hit me on the back and another on the cheek. Soon, I felt that I was being pelted with the big drops of water. Mother hurried up the line and we ran toward the entrance to our tunnel.

By the time we ducked into the warmth and safety of our passageway, Louisa was crying and Annabelle was complaining bitterly about her wet fur. Sue Mary just giggled and Frisk, who was last, pushed from the rear of the line. He was still exposed to the wetness.

Mother checked for enemies that might have taken cover in our house, as carefully as she could under the circumstances, then led us down toward our nest. Quite suddenly a terrible rumbling up above us made us all dive into our bed and cover our heads in fright. When it finally ceased we looked out, still trembling with fear.

"What was it?" Frisk whispered.

"Thunder," said Father.

"Will it come down here?" he asked again and we all crowded a bit closer to one another.

"No," laughed Father. "Thunder doesn't come down here. It comes with the rain. But it stays in the sky with lightning."

"Who's Lightning?" asked Annabelle for all of us.

"Bright flashes of light," Father explained. "Thunder and lightning always seem to travel together."

"You've seen them?" asked Sue Mary, her small eyes round with disbelief and fright.

"I've seen lightning," said Father

"It didn't hurt you?" It was my turn for a question.

"No-o. But sometimes it can be dangerous I've heard."

"What does it do?" Frisk prompted.

"Well sometimes lightning starts prairie fires."

"What does that do? Is that dangerous?"

"Very dangerous."

"What does it do? Fire?"

"Fire eats everything in its path. All of the grasses, even the roots. The sagebrush and tumbleweed. Everything is gone after a prairie fire. It is very difficult to find anything at all to eat."

We were all too frightened by the thought to ask any more questions. Fire must be a dreadful foe— and fire was the result of lightning.

Overhead thunder rumbled again. We snuggled in closer to one another. I didn't like the smell of the wet fur, but I was afraid to leave the safety of the family.

We lay there, shivering and shaking, still wet and cold, and then Father and Mother joined us and began to clean us up and dry us off. Even thunder didn't sound so menacing when they were near.

Gradually we were dried and just as gradually thunder seemed to get further and further away from our home. Soon it was just a rumble in the distance.

"The storm is moving off," I heard Father say to Mother and I took great comfort in his words and snuggled up closely to Frisk. There really didn't seem to be anything to worry about. I shut my eyes and prepared to catch some much needed sleep.

Chapter Five

Growing Up

The next morning when we left our nest there were puddles everywhere. I had never seen so much water before but Father said that he had seen times when the rain had filled the rivers so full that they overran their banks and spilled out onto the prairies. I began to wish for such a rain until I saw the look on Mother's face. It seemed that the water was something to be feared.

The morning sun sent warm fingers earthward and soon our whole world seemed to be hazy with shivering steam. I was so fascinated by it that I just sat and watched—forgetting that I was very hungry.

Soon the warmth of the day made the mist disappear and much to my dismay the puddles began to disappear also. Where they went I will never know. Father said that most of the rain soaked right into the ground, but some of it, he said, evaporated.

Evaporated was a word that I didn't understand. "What's e-e-vorp-ated?" I asked.

Father smiled. "E-va-por-ated," he said carefully.

"Yeah—that," I said, not willing to try the difficult word again.

"Well," said Father, wriggling his nose, "evaporate means—to—to disappear. The rain falls down from the clouds—then it—it goes back up into the air and into the clouds again."

He seemed happy with his explanation.

I looked heavenward. I couldn't see any clouds. For the first time in my life I was a bit skeptical about an answer from Father. I didn't want to hurt him so I just nodded my head as though his explanation was perfectly sound.

"When the clouds get enough rain back up there," Father went on, "they will send it back down to earth again."

It sounded awfully silly to me. Up, down. Up, down. Why would they want to do that? I asked Father.

"Why?"

"Why?" repeated Father. "Because. That's why. That's just the way it is."

"But you said we need rain to make the grass grow," I reminded Father.

"We do."

"Then why does it just go back up?"

"The grass has enough. See. It's still wet."

"How can it go back up and water the grass too?"

"It doesn't all go back up," said Father. "Just what's left over."

"How does it know how much is left over," I persisted, "and how much needs to stay to water the grass?"

"What goes into the ground waters the grass; what goes back up waters the clouds," replied Father.

"But—but—," I began. "You said that sometimes it rains even more."

"It does—and sometimes it rains less."

"Then if it's not always the same—how does it know how much should stay and how much should go?" I puzzled.

Father turned from me slightly and took a mouthful of the juicy prairie grasses. "Why don't you have some breakfast?" he asked me and I knew that he had had enough questions for one morning.

I moved away, then stopped to look up again at the sky. I still couldn't see any clouds and most of the water had already disappeared, though it still felt wet and 'squishy' underfoot. I shook my head. Father was a very wise man but I somehow knew that he was a bit off-track on this one.

I moved over toward Frisk and began to share his breakfast. He didn't complain. Frisk was good about sharing.

I was just beginning to enjoy my meal when a sharp bark came from the nearest sentry. I froze mid-step, my foot suspended, my whole body tense with awareness. It was the first time that I had heard the warning signal but Mother had grilled us so thoroughly that I knew exactly what to do.

It seemed like I stood there forever but I guess it was a very short time. I could sense and smell my family members about me but I didn't dare to even turn my head to see what they were doing. I knew instinctively that they had all frozen into position as well.

How long, I was asking myself, how long did Mother say I was to be perfectly still before I could go on with my eating? I was very aware now of just how hungry I was.

Then came another sharp bark, and I knew *that* signal as well. That meant that we were all to dive for the safety of our tunnel just as fast as our short legs could get us there.

Without even looking around I began to run. I hadn't known that I could run so fast, but for some reason unknown to me, I was suddenly scared to death.

Somewhere, in some direction, I knew not which, was danger. An enemy lurked nearby, seeking one of us for his morning breakfast. Perhaps he was as hungry as I was, only he didn't wish to feed on the prairie grasses. He wished to feed on me.

I was in no hurry to become someone's breakfast. There was too much of the world that I hadn't even seen yet. I ran. Tail held high and head tucked down low, I ran. And all around me was the patter of other running feet and the whisper of prairie grass as small bodies scurried through it on the way to their homes.

Just as I neared our entrance, another sentry gave the cry of alarm. That really frightened me. I tried to increase my speed, running blindly in my hurry to reach the nest.

It was then that my feet tangled up in some weird way and I flipped end over end, sailing through the air and landing on my back with a 'thunk' that knocked the wind right out of me.

My heart was hammering in my chest and my throat was so dry with fright that I couldn't have even cried out if I had tried to.

I righted myself as quickly as I could, shook my head to clear the cobwebs and headed for the first open door that I spied.

I was half tumbling, half running, down the

passageway, when an angry voice stopped me in my tracks.

"Halt!" he screamed. "What are you doing here?"

I skidded to a stop, blinking my eyes. I didn't recognize the voice. Certainly it wasn't Mother or Father. I began to wonder what this stranger was doing in our tunnel. Then he screamed at me again, and this time he was coming toward me.

"What are you doing in here," I asked, "speak up!"

It was then that my nose began to work again. This was not our tunnel. No wonder it was not Mother's or Father's voice. In my confusion I had dived into someone else's home by mistake.

Mother had warned us about intruding. If there was any strict rule in our town, it was the respect for another person's privacy. No one—I mean no one—would tolerate intrusion.

"I didn't mean—," I began, but he was getting awfully close to me and he looked so big and so mad.

"I fell—I was running and I fell and I got switched in my directions. I meant to go home."

"Home? This is my home."

"I know. I'm sorry. Truly I—."

"Out," he screamed at me. "Out."

He was almost to me now and I began to back up, fearful that he might reach out and nip me soundly.

"I will," I agreed. "I will. Just as soon as the sentry says we can leave the—."

"You'll leave now."

"But—but the—the danger isn't passed."

"Out!" he cried again.

"But—."

He did nip me then. Right on the shoulder. It

hurt. It hurt real bad. I could see then that I was in just as much danger in the home of the stranger as I would likely be outside. I began to back my way out of the tunnelway as quickly as I could.

As I scurried, my thoughts ran ahead of me. Might the enemy be right at the top of the hole waiting for me to stick my neck out? Had he been listening to the conversation? Would he know I was coming?

And if I did make it safely out of the entrance, where would I go? In my confusion I had no idea of what direction to run for safety.

I couldn't even stop to be cautious. The big, angry neighbor was right behind me. I had no desire to be nipped again. Shutting my eyes tightly so that I wouldn't see the enemy that I was sure was waiting there to grab me in strong teeth, I thrust myself forward, running for all I was worth, with no direction in mind.

And then I heard the most welcome sound that I had ever heard. It was Father's voice and he was calling me. I shifted direction and opened my eyes. There was Father, standing on his hind legs, beckoning me to hasten to the tunnel.

I ran. I ran as fast as I could. I was almost to the entrance when Father suddenly disappeared. All that I saw was a flip of his tail and he was gone from my view and then I saw something else too. A great shadow crossed over me and I thought for a minute that Father's clouds were back soaking up the extra rain again. I turned my head just slightly so that I could look upward and instead of clouds I saw a big bird on enormous wings, swooping toward the earth.

For some reason I understood it all then. This

was one of the enemies that I had been warned about. This was why the sentries had cried. This was why Father had disappeared with a whisk of his tail and this was who wanted me for breakfast.

With a final burst of speed I flung myself forward and tumbled into the opening of our passageway just as the woosh of wings passed over my head and the hungry, long talons grasped at empty air.

I heard the bird screech in anger. It rang in my ears almost as loud as the thumping sound of my own heart. I lay there stunned, not sure if I was safe or not yet and then Father was nuzzling me and bringing me back to my senses.

"Are you alright?" he was asking anxiously.

I couldn't speak. I couldn't even nod.

Mother pushed forward then. She ran her nose over my cheek and shoulder. Already she had found the tender spot where I had been so viciously nipped.

"You're hurt," she cried in a worried voice.

"He's fine," said Father. "It's just a nip and it will heal. He's safe, that's the main thing."

I was becoming more aware of my circumstances now. Father was right. I was safe. And that *was* the main thing.

I tried to get my feet back under me again. My head was still whirling and I felt nauseated and dizzy.

"Come dear," said Mother. "We need to get away from the entrance. Come."

Father gave me some assistance and we made our way down to the nest where I was greeted by Frisk and the girls. Annabelle was crying and Sue Mary looked as white as I felt. They all welcomed me and I suddenly began to enjoy it all—now that I was really safe, that is.

I lay down and let them all fuss over me. Mother was busy cleaning up the wound and making sure that I was as comfortable as I could be. Father was nearby fretting and soothing, both at the same time. All of my siblings were asking questions and exclaiming over my close call. All but Louisa that is. She was sleeping in spite of all of the commotion.

At length things seemed to settle down some. My heart was back to its usual rate. Annabelle had dried all of her tears. Mother seemed to feel that she had done all she could for my injury. Sue Mary had lost her paleness and Frisk was ready to talk about something other than my near calamity.

Mother turned to me then. "That was a close call," she said. "I'm sure you understand now what Father and I have been trying to teach you."

Just thinking about it made me start to shiver again.

"You've learned, first-hand, two very important lessons today," went on Mother. "And I do hope that you never experience them again."

I nodded. I hoped so too.

"One is that you never, never intrude into someone else's home. No one will treat such an intrusion lightly."

"Why?" asked Frisk. "Why was he so mean? Flick meant no harm. He wasn't even going to stay."

"We all are very protective of our homes," said Father. "Our homes are meant for us—only. We guard them with our lives. We do not want intruders. Our family must be safe here. Other animals could harm our children, steal our food or—."

"But Flick wasn't gonna do any of those things," cut in Sue Mary. "He just wanted to hide."

"But Flick must remember that we check our homes with our sense of smell. We can tell immediately when we enter our tunnel if it has been visited by anyone other than our own family. Flick's presence in the passageway has mixed-up that orderliness. His scent is now there. The family might even have to move. Build a new home. Unless they can repair or clean out the passageway as far as Flick intruded. They just wouldn't feel safe there anymore."

I hadn't known that it was *that* important. *That* complicated. I was sorry that it had happened. I certainly hadn't intended to destroy the safety of our neighbors. I hung my head.

"I'll talk with the Dickerwicks tomorrow," said Father. "Talk won't mend their home but at least we will apologize and explain how it happened."

"It was unfortunate," said Mother, "but not intentional. Might it be a lesson to all of you."

The whole nest of young were very solemn— except the sleeping Louisa.

"You also learned," went on Mother, "that a hawk's talons are greatly to be feared. I still don't know how you ever made it to safety. They seldom miss."

She reached over and nuzzled me again and there were tears in her eyes.

I was quite willing to agree with Mother. I had learned two very important lessons—and like her— I hoped that I never had to experience them again.

Chapter Six

Sowing The Seed

As the days went by, Father and Mother allowed us more and more freedom. I could still feel Mother's sharp eye on me though and more than occasionally her voice reached out to caution me or give me a bit of good, sound, motherly advice. It made me feel safe and cared for—but, regardless of that, I still liked to push the boundaries just as far as I could.

I soon established myself as the curious one of the family. Father would scowl and Mother would shake her head with a very worried look in her eyes. "Your curiosity is going to get you in trouble, Flick," she often said, and then she would add in a solemn voice, "I do hope and pray that it won't be serious trouble."

Then her eyes would lift to the sky or swing all around the village as though she expected a hawk to be poised above me, or a bobcat to be crouched ready to spring.

I would laugh at Mother, give my tail a quick flip and scurry off to see what else I could discover about our village world.

Time after time I sat and gazed off into the distance. The prairie grasses seemed to stretch on and on forever, waving gently when the breeze stirred them, and whipping and bending in the strong gusts of the more violent winds.

Beyond the grasses were hills and rocks and the vague outline of what Father said was trees. I had never seen a tree. Not up close that is. Boy, did I wish that I could get closer for a real good look. They looked like they would be much bigger in size than the grass or sagebrush. I wondered how they would taste. Would they be sweet and tender or bitter like the root that I tried one day when Mother wasn't looking?

I hadn't liked the root at all. No wonder Mother had said not to eat it. It was bitter and it made my tummy feel funny, too. In fact, I had gone back to the nest and tried to sleep, not feeling like eating anymore.

Mother had wondered about it but, apart from coming to see how I was, she left me pretty much alone. I was glad. I really didn't feel like talking and I sure didn't want to have to tell Mother the truth about my disobedience. It wasn't that I wished to disobey. It was just that I was curious to know 'why' we weren't to eat that root.

Well, I found out—for sure. I would never try it again. Not even a nibble.

But I pushed that all aside, and for about the hundredth time, gazed out at the distant hills again. How exciting they looked. Surely there would be so much to explore there. Perhaps even different, delicious things to eat. There must be just hundreds of places to hide from an enemy. And the homes that one could build in all of that space, would be fantastic.

I must have had that far-away look in my eye.

"Flick!"

It was Mother's voice.

"Don't even think it!"

Could Mother read minds?

I shook my head slightly and with a sigh moved away from Mother and began feeding on some roots that were half-hidden by a jagged rock. They were delicious. The problem was that they were also hard to get at. The rock stuck out this way and that way and bound them in here and there.

I tried to push the rock aside but it was too heavy. I worked my way around it, shoving first one way then another, but no matter what direction I tried, it still refused to move.

At last I just gave up and shoved my nose in just as close against it as I could, nibbling at the roots I could get my teeth on. My tongue helped some. With its help I was able to reach a few more stems that I could pull up with my teeth and then nibble on the roots. They were so sweet and so tender. I assumed it was because they had been so sheltered by the rock and hadn't been exposed to the rigors of the hot sun and sweeping wind.

All the way around the rock I worked, pulling and tearing, scratching away with the sharp claws of my front feet and wrapping my tongue around stems to jerk them up. It was exhausting work—but worth it. The roots were the best that I had ever tasted.

I could still see a few more stocks but they were almost impossible to reach. It irked me. I pushed and shoved with my whole body. I tried using my front feet to tug the rock away. I leaned against the

rock and put all of my weight against the stubborn outcropping. Nothing worked. I could still taste the sweetness of the roots in my mouth and I wanted more. I wanted to eat until the very last root had been devoured. I thought of going to get Frisk. With his help I might be able to move the stubborn, resistant piece of rock.

But I hesitated. If I called Frisk I would also need to share my find with him. Besides, now that I knew how good the roots were, I would search around all the nearby rocks for other plants of the same kind. Maybe our area was filled with them and other town residents hadn't discovered yet how good they were. Well, I sure wouldn't be the one to share the secret. At least not until I had my fill.

I put my nose against the miserable rock and pushed with all my might. My tongue reached out to try to coax a stem into my mouth where my sharp, strong teeth could get a grasp on it. I couldn't quite reach. I dug in my hind feet and pushed harder, squirming against the resistance before me.

Then with a sharp cry I sprang backward. I had tried too hard. I had pushed too hard. I had squirmed just a bit too much. The jagged edge of the rock had cut right across my tender nose.

I couldn't see the blood but when I flicked out my tongue I could taste it. It had a strange, sweet, metallic taste. I licked at it again. The open cut strung when I ran my tongue over it. I had no idea how bad it might be. I supposed that I should go find Mother so that she could care for it, but I was a little embarrassed about my situation. What would everyone think when I ran around with a scar on my nose?

I knew one thing that they would think. They'd think that I'd had my nose where it didn't belong. That's what they would think. They would probably also think that some other town citizen had smartly smacked it, either with teeth or claw.

It was embarrassing alright. It was also painful. It stung. I licked it again. It was still bleeding. I really should go find Mother.

But if I went to Mother, she'd ask how it happened and I would have to explain. She would likely even want to see the rock and examine the roots I had been eating. I had the feeling that if the roots had grown in that particular spot, they would grow there again. If they did grow there, I wanted to be the one to find them. If I showed Mother, she would share them with the whole family. There wouldn't be enough to go around, I knew that. I wasn't even full yet. How could a family of seven feast on the short supply?

I didn't go to Mother. I stayed as far away from her as I dared. I ate other roots and grasses until my tummy was full. They weren't nearly as tasty. I kept thinking about the tender roots by the rock, but I didn't go back. Not yet. But I would. I knew that.

It seemed a long time until the wound stopped dribbling blood. It didn't bleed hard—just little drop by little drop. I would have to put out my tongue and lick it away. Then I would go on with my eating.

The wound was in such an awkward spot. I hadn't realized before just how much I needed my nose as I fed. Now, I seemed to bump it every time I reached for another bite.

I made sure that I stayed away from the other members of my family while I waited for my nose to stop bleeding. Eventually it did, but it still stung. By the time it had stopped, I had eaten enough. It had quit two or three times prior to that, but I had bumped it and started it up again. I was thankful when I felt full. It meant that I could quit eating and go take a nap. I hoped that I would be all alone in the nest. The thought of siblings banging against my sore nose as they tossed in sleep, made me shudder.

When I arrived at the entrance I found Mother there. I wasn't sure if she was waiting or just sunning herself. She looked rather sleepy. In fact her eyes were barely open but I saw her keen nose began to twitch, then her eyes flew open wide.

I swung away from her and pretended to be studying the distant hills again. I hoped that she hadn't noticed my scratched up nose.

"How'd you hurt yourself?" she asked me.

"I'm okay—," I started but she cut me short.

"I smell blood," she said. "What did you do?"

I turned to face her then and heard her little gasp.

"Oh, Flick," she began in a pleading voice. "When will you learn not to be so curious—so nosy?"

"I wasn't—," I started and hardly knew how to explain.

"Then how did that happen?"

"I was eating and cut it on a rock." It did sound pretty silly.

I saw the doubt in Mother's eyes. She didn't say anything, just looked at me.

"I did!" I insisted. "Just ask—." I floundered. There was no one to ask. I had been all alone. I wondered if she was going to tell me that she didn't believe my story.

"Why didn't you come to me?" she asked instead.

"I—I—it wasn't that bad," I stammered. I knew that my actions and words were making my story seem even more unbelievable but I couldn't tell Mother the whole truth without her thinking that I was terribly selfish. Mother had tried hard to teach us to share.

"It looks to me like a rather nasty scratch," she said almost sternly. "And you have a good deal of dirt in it. It could become infected."

"I got the dirt in it while eating," I said. "every time I went to take another bite I bumped it."

"Yes," she observed, tilting her head slightly, "it is in an awkward place. I expect you'll bump it many times over the next few days."

I hadn't thought of that.

"So you aren't going to own up to how you came by it?"

I just stood there, saying nothing, trying to think of some satisfactory explanation. I could just explain the whole thing to Mother and then she would know I was telling the truth—even if she did give me a lecture on my selfishness. I started to open my mouth and then I thought again of the succulent roots. I was just sure that they would grow again, and in just a few days—by the time my nose healed even—I might be able to feast on them again.

I shrugged my shoulders carelessly and avoided Mother's eyes. "I did tell you," I said. "I already did."

"I see," said Mother, but I could tell by the tone of her voice that she didn't see at all. Not really.

She nodded her head toward the entrance. "You'd better go on down," she said, "I'll see what I can do to get it cleaned up."

She did. I didn't feel that she was quite as gentle as usual. After she was done I curled up in a corner of the nest and tried to go to sleep. Why didn't you explain? I kept asking myself. But I didn't have a good answer. It was plain selfishness, I knew that, but even I couldn't figure why I relished the tasty roots so much that I would forfeit Mother's trust to have them all to myself.

"Maybe it will sort itself out," I reasoned. "When the roots no longer grow, then I'll explain."

I wasn't sure how long that would be, and I wasn't sure what other consequences there might be to pay in the meantime, but I pushed all of that aside and tried to get some rest.

Chapter Seven

Games

In the days that followed I took a good deal of teasing, you can be sure of that. They dubbed me Scar Nose and the younger kids would stand off to the side when I made my appearance each morning and chant after me, "Scar Nose, Scar Nose, Sticks in his nose, Now the scar shows." I hated the song. I guess I hated the kids, too, but I tried not to let them know it.

I would often feel Mother studying me to catch my reaction to the teasing. I tried not to let her know how it bothered me and went right on with whatever I was doing.

The older fellas were curious about my sore nose too but they sorta seemed to get the notion that I had been in some kind of dispute with someone. They kept making comments like, "What does the other guy look like?" and "Are you the licker or the lickee?" At first it bothered me and then I began to realize that I had reached a certain kind of hero status in their eyes and I began to rather enjoy it. I was almost sorry when my nose began to improve.

Now that we were allowed more freedom, we also became acquainted with more of our neighbors. All around us were youngsters our age. It was great to have so many playmates. Often we hurried as quickly as we could to eat our meal so that we would have more playing time.

Our favorite game was tag, but we also enjoyed hide-and-seek and our own version of leap frog.

Playing games is a good way to get to know your neighbors quickly. We soon learned who the bullies were, who the considerate, who the shy, who the witty or the outspoken. We also learned very quickly just who made the games fun to play and who made them seem more like a war. We tried to avoid those 'whos' but they were awfully hard to avoid. They were always the first ones there, already yelling "Not it" before the rest of us had even had time to discuss the game we wished to play.

Sandy Mallorstock was the biggest bully of all. And he was always the first one to show up yelling, "Not it for tag," or "Not it for hide-and-seek," before the rest of us had even said, "Let's play tag," or "Let's play hide-and-seek." Then he spent his time tormenting and teasing whoever was 'it.' No one would chase him. So he made faces and name-called and tripped runners and pushed whoever he could push. Nobody liked him. Not even the girls.

But he never missed a game. No matter how we tried to quietly organize a game without his finding out, we never were successful. We finally just gave up and played our games in spite of his many interruptions.

Pepe Fotterby was my best friend. He was the son of the sentry that was often on duty near our house. Of course there were many sentries. They took turns so that they might have time to eat and sleep and groom themselves and spend time with family and visit neighbors and all those things.

Pepe was not at all like his father. He was small and lean and wiry. He could run faster than any of the neighborhood fellas and jump farther and higher than even the bigger boys. He did everything with a big grin. Pepe enjoyed life and just being around him made life more fun and exciting. I was glad that Pepe was my friend.

Mother and Father were pleased that I spent my time with Pepe. In spite of being a fun-loving fellow, he was polite and well-mannered and always obeyed his parents. I think that they were hoping that a good measure of his attitude would rub off on me.

I liked Pepe a lot. I did chafe a bit at times that he seemed to accept his world just as it was handed to him. He never seemed one bit curious to know what was beyond the limits set out for us by our parents.

I did wonder about the world, and I did wish I could find out what it was really like, but I knew if ever there was a time that I would try to find out, I wouldn't be taking Pepe along with me. I was sure that Sandy would be more than willing to go but I wasn't too sure that Sandy was the kind of company that I wanted.

Day after day I kept checking the spot where the delicious roots grew by the rock. I thought at times that there appeared to be a greenish cast to the sandy soil but no young sprouts appeared.

My sore nose began to heal. That was good news. It had been so miserable to live with. I did, just as Mother had predicted, bump it often when I tried to root out grasses. It always hurt and a few times I even started it bleeding again.

But still I refused to tell my secret. I was sure that one day soon the tasty roots would be there again and I didn't want to have to share them with anyone. I hadn't even told Frisk or Pepe about them.

I knew that Mother was still suspicious. I knew that she kept an even closer eye on me. I had to be extra careful when I sneaked off to check out my own private patch.

One day I was coming back from making sure that no one else had found my secret spot when Mother looked up from her eating and called me over.

"Where've you been?" she asked me pleasantly enough.

I shrugged and turned slightly away from her.

"Just—just here and there," I said evasively.

"You haven't been meeting with Sandy, have you?"

Mother knew Sandy's reputation and I knew that she didn't want my name to be linked with his.

I didn't even like Sandy but I didn't tell Mother that.

"No," I said instead, "honest!"

I could tell that Mother wanted to believe me. I could tell that she was also hoping that I would go on with my explanation about where I had been and what I had been doing. I didn't. I still wasn't willing to give up my patch of tasty roots.

"Who were you with?" she continued.

"No one. I was alone." I went on to declare forcefully, stubbornly, "honest!"

Mother looked doubtful.

"I thought that you liked to play the games."

"I do."

"The other boys were all playing tag. I saw them. That is, all but you and Sandy."

So that was it! Sandy had been missing from the game, too. Could I tell Mother that the boys always tried to play without Sandy but they had just never managed to be successful before? I couldn't help but wonder how they had gotten away with it this time. My eyes must have shown some kind of question for Mother looked at me. I had the feeling that she read the surprise on my face as fear because I had been caught.

"So where were you?" she asked again and I knew that she was really giving me one last chance to clear myself.

"Alone," I insisted. "Alone. And I wasn't in any trouble either. Honest!"

I think that Mother hated to hear me use the word 'honest' when she was so sure that I was anything but. Well, I guess I wasn't totally honest when you come to think of it. I mean, I hadn't told Mother the whole truth. I just hadn't lied.

The fact that I was selfishly trying to save the roots for myself wouldn't have set well with Mother, but I was smart enough to know that she would forgive my selfishness far more easily than she would forgive lying.

The tears were stinging my eyes as I flung my words at Mother, "Look! I was not with Sandy. Maybe he wasn't playing but I don't know where he was. And I don't care either. I was alone—just like I said and I—."

"Son!"

Father's sharp voice stopped me. I hadn't seen

him come up beside me.

"That is no way to talk to your mother," he said firmly. "Now I suggest that if you can't behave in a more courteous manner you go to the den."

He wasn't finished with what he had to say but I started off anyway. It wasn't fair. I hadn't done anything. At least I sure hadn't done what they thought I'd done—whatever that was, but here I was in trouble anyway just because I wouldn't tell them the whole story.

I began to question my own choices. Surely roots, even delicious roots, weren't worth all of the trouble that they were causing me.

And then I thought of the roots again and quickly changed my mind. They were. They really were. I decided to just tough it out and hope that they grew in a hurry.

If I wasn't known to be so curious about everything, I told myself, Mother wouldn't be so suspicious. She'd just let me go like she does Frisk without even getting worried about such little things.

Deep in my heart I knew that Mother's worry was prompted by love. She was concerned about me, I knew that. Well, sometimes love could be a bit too protective for comfort. I wished that she didn't care quite so much.

I went back down to the den and curled up alone in our nest. I was angry. I was angry with the roots for not growing faster. I was angry with Mother for not trusting me. I was angry with Father for taking Mother's part and I was even a bit angry with myself for not telling them the truth.

I was missing the afternoon feeding. I was missing the games of the fellows and I was even missing seeing the exciting events that were taking place in our neighborhood.

It just didn't seem fair.

I hadn't been there too long when a very full Louisa joined me in the nest.

"How come you're here?" she asked, knowing that I never spent time napping when I could be doing something else instead. I hardly answered. Just sort of snarled, "Father."

"Oh," said Louisa, in a tight little voice.

We were silent for a time and then she continued.

"What did you do?"

"Nothin'."

"Nothin'?"

"That's right. Nothin'."

"I didn't know Father sent us to the nest for doing nothin'," said Louisa.

I remembered then just why Father had sent me in.

"He thought I was smart-mouthing Mother."

"Weren't you?"

I shrugged, but kept silent.

"Well?" said Louisa.

"Maybe—some. But I didn't mean to be."

"Did you tell Mother that? Say you were sorry?" asked Louisa.

Come to think of it, I hadn't. I hadn't even thought to apologize. I was too annoyed at being questioned.

Perhaps that was why Father had sent me in to bed.

Louisa had talked for long enough. Her eyes were already getting droopy. She yawned. I wasn't about to keep her from her sleep. Besides, she had already said quite enough as far as I was concerned.

"Maybe you should have," she said sleepily and then curled right up against me and fell immediately to sleep.

"Maybe," I mumbled, but I knew that Louisa didn't hear me.

I vowed that I would try to remember to do that the next time that Mother and I had a confrontation. Then I, too, curled up and went to sleep. For some reason it didn't seem quite so bad to be sent to bed when Louisa was there to share the nest with me.

Chapter Eight

Exploring

The roots didn't seem to be growing back. I checked on them whenever I could sneak away but they never did appear again. I was sorry about that. I guess they just grew from the root, not from seed, and when I had eaten them I had pulled them up and devoured them completely.

I tried to put them out of my mind and concentrate on other things.

There were certainly many things to concentrate on. Spring had passed well into summer. The hot sandy prairie land simmered in the afternoon sunshine. The clouds gathered their moisture and periodically dumped it back to earth, then busied themselves taking it back up again, just as Father had explained. The young of the prairie animals were growing bigger and the baby birds had become feathered and left their nests. Each day held so many things to see and to learn. I turned my thoughts from the roots and began to get excited again about other things.

One thing had always puzzled me. At the end of

each day the big red ball of sun dipped into the west, snuggled up into the hills and pulled the blanket of darkness over himself and all of the critters. Father said that night was a dangerous time and all of us had to be safely tucked away in our bed before darkness descended.

Yet when I questioned Father about the night, he knew very little about it. He had never been out at night. I couldn't help but wonder why he accepted all of the stories as fact when he had never checked them out for himself. I vowed that sometime, somehow, I was going to check out the night. In the meantime, I decided that I should learn all about the night that I could.

"What is the night like?" I asked Mother and Father.

"It's black," said Father.

"It's dangerous," promptly added Mother. "It's filled with enemies."

"The hawk?"

"No, I understand the hawk sleeps at night just as we do," said Father.

"The coyote?" I asked.

"I really don't know," Father admitted. "I have never been in the night to find out. But I've heard that there are many creatures that hunt at night. And they aren't looking for prairie grasses either."

"You mean us?" Sue Mary's eyes got big as she asked the question.

"They would like to find us—yes," said Father. "Only we outsmart them. We go to our beds.

Sue Mary shivered. I was quite sure that she wouldn't be checking out the night.

I didn't say any more. I didn't want to make anyone suspicious.

That night when we went to bed I made sure that I slept the closest to the tunnel passageway. I didn't want to be crawling over bodies when I sneaked from the bed.

It seemed to take forever for everyone to get to sleep. I was afraid that morning would come before I could peek outside. Besides, I just knew that there were all kinds of exciting things to see out there and I was missing a good part of it.

At last I heard Father's heavy snores and Mother's even breathing and I eased myself away from Frisk and crept quietly and noiselessly up the passageway. As I went the excitement mounted within me. The nearer I got to the top, the more excited I became. I could hardly wait to see the outside world at night.

At first I was disappointed. It was so black out without the brightness of the sun that I could scarcely see anything. I sat at the entrance to our home, blinking and winking and trying to get my eyes to focus more properly. It was of little use. My eyes were just not made for the darkness. Then as I sat there confused and frustrated, a light peeked out from behind a cloud and I could see a bit more clearly.

I did remember my training and checked carefully before leaving the entrance. Now that I was out and free to explore the night world I wasn't quite sure where to go.

A shiver ran all along my backbone. It was rather scary at that.

I decided to see what I could find to eat. At night, with no neighbors around, I decided that I wouldn't need to be concerned with boundaries. I could eat whatever and wherever I pleased and so I set about finding myself the most tempting grasses and roots.

"Wouldn't it be wonderful if I found some of the special roots," I was telling myself when I felt more than saw a shadow pass over my head.

My first instinct was to duck, and then from habit I listened for the bark of the sentry. It was then that I reminded myself that I hadn't stopped at the exit to check the locations of the sentries, and then I smiled to myself in the darkness. There *wouldn't be* any sentries. Not a one. They, too, were all sleeping soundly in their beds.

My smile quickly changed to concern. If there weren't any sentries, then who would stand on guard for me as I fed? I had never had to worry about that before.

"I'll be my own sentry," I told myself. "I can watch as well as eat."

But I didn't really do much eating. There was too much to see. I couldn't believe how different the world looked by night.

A slight movement off to my right made me freeze in my tracks. Thankfully it was only Jack, the large rabbit who also occupied our part of the prairie. I had never really spoken to him before but to my surprise he looked my way and nodded.

I felt encouraged by that and decided to move just a bit closer. I didn't dare venture too close. I knew all about boundaries and feeding rights.

"Hi," I said rather hesitantly.

His whiskers twitched as he nibbled at the mouthful of grass he was devouring. He spoke around it. "Hi."

I didn't know what to say after the 'hi' so I just sat there wondering what to do next.

He broke the silence.

"How come you're not in bed? Thought prairie dogs sleep at night."

"We do. I mean, well—they do. I—I couldn't sleep. Didn't want to sleep," I corrected.

"Everyone needs sleep," said Jack.

"Oh, I'll sleep. I'm not staying out all night. Just long enough to—to."

I wanted to stay to see what it was like, but that seemed rather childish to someone like Jack who was out whenever he wanted to be.

"So when do you sleep?" I asked him.

"Whenever I like. I take naps. Sleep awhile—feed awhile."

It sounded like a real good arrangement to me. I wondered why we didn't do it that way. Then we would be able to see both worlds.

Jack must have read my mind. "Your eyes aren't made for the night," he quickly informed me. "You'd never see the enemies coming up behind you."

The way that Jack said it made me shiver and I quickly swung my head around to check to be sure that one wasn't sneaking up on me now. I guess I expected to see a tall dark object just ready to pounce. Jack began to laugh. He thought the whole thing uproariously funny.

"Loosen up, Dog," he told me. "Now that you're out, enjoy it."

I nodded, but my smile was a bit weak.

"This your first time out at night?" he asked me and when I nodded he went on.

"Well, what do you want to know about it? I've been out at nights since I was no more than a bunny."

Jack laughed at his joke. He obviously thought

that he had quite a wit.

"Well—," I said, hesitantly. I did not want to offend Jack. I realized that he was my unexpected source of information. Without him I would have learned very little about the night—even though I was standing in it. "What's that?" and I pointed up.

"That? That's the moon. Haven't you seen the moon before?"

I shook my head. "I thought maybe the sun was going out, or faded or something," I said and Jack laughed again. I guess he thought that I was funny, too.

"Sun going out," he laughed. "That's crazy."

Then I noticed all of the smaller lights in the sky. They seemed to be flashing all above us.

"What are those?" I asked.

It looked to me like someone had punched the sky full of tiny holes and the sun was spilling through all of them.

"Stars," said Jack.

"All of them?"

Jack guffawed again. I was afraid he would awaken my parents; he was so loud.

"All of them," he informed me. "And you're only seeing a part of them too. I've seen them when the sky was almost solid in spots, they were so thick."

"Really?"

"Really."

"Where do they go?"

"To bed I suppose. Guess they're like me, instead of like you. Guess they feed for awhile and then nap for awhile."

"Oh!" It sounded perfectly logical to me.

"Wanna look around?" offered Jack. "I've had enough to eat for now. I could take you."

"Sure," I said and took an excited step forward and then I remembered the shadow that had passed over my head. I looked up, then looked around. It was scary in the night. Really scary.

"Aw, don't be a scaredy-cat," said Jack, noticing my hesitation. "I've been out at night ever since—."

"You were a bunny," I finished for him and waited for Jack to laugh. He did.

I pushed my fears to the back of my mind and moved forward with Jack.

"What—what animals are out at night?" I asked him, thinking that he should know.

"Oh, coyotes, badgers, bobcats—."

"Snakes?"

"Yeah, snakes."

Jack had listed a good number of creatures on my enemy list. It made me shiver but I was determined not to let it scare me—too much.

"What about hawks?" I went on, as though it didn't really matter much.

"Most of them feed in the daytime."

"Yeah, I know," I said with a shiver. "On prairie dogs."

Jack laughed again though I really couldn't see anything so funny about it.

"On rabbits, too," he said. "When they can catch them that is. Me, I've outrun more than one hawk in my day."

"Outran them?" I said doubting his story, "How?" I knew a little about how fast a hawk could swoop.

"Just duck and dodge," said Jack and swung his shoulders this way and that to demonstrate.

"Well, I hope we won't need to do any ducking and dodging tonight," I said with a husky voice. I wasn't built like a rabbit.

Jack took me on a tour all around our town. He even offered to take me to the outcropping of rock in the distance but I said we'd better leave it for another night and he agreed. I wasn't as fast as Jack and I slowed him down considerably.

At last we agreed that I'd better get back to the nest and get some sleep before morning came. Already the grass was getting wet with the dews of night and my feet were damp and I was getting cold.

"I'll see you home," Jack said, and I was about to protest that I could find my way just fine when the moon dipped behind a cloud again.

I could hardly see at all then and Jack realized that when I tripped over a rock that was in my path.

He was hopping along beside me, both of us giving full attention to where I was placing my feet when there was a scurry behind us. I swung around to stare into the darkness, the fur on my neck standing up in fright. I could see nothing.

Jack must have seen something with his night-time eyes. He gave me a rough shove and yelled, "Run Flick! Run!"

I still didn't know what I was running from but I didn't wait to ask. I just made a dash for what I hoped was the entrance to our tunnel and ran as fast as my short legs could take me.

The moon chose that moment to make its appearance again and when I looked back over my shoulders I saw a huge animal with vicious looking teeth and shining eyes—right on my tail. I was sure he was just ready to take a snap at the rear of me when Jack dashed between us and diverted his attention. The animal swung from me just long enough for me to gain a bit of ground. Then he changed his mind and was off after Jack in a flash. I could hear them both smashing through the prairie grasses as they made their way across the bumpy ground, Jack zig-zagging his way between prairie dog mounds just as he had demonstrated.

I was still frozen in my tracks, shivering at my close call when I heard another noise. I looked up and there was another animal, coming right toward me. I thought that I would die of fright, but I somehow managed to get my feet going again and was off as fast as I could go toward our entranceway.

I thought I would never make it. And I very nearly didn't. Just as I slipped into the passage I heard the click of teeth on my heels. I felt them brush against my body. It threw me off balance somewhat but they were just a second too late to stop me.

I tumbled down the entranceway, fighting for breath and seeking for refuge. I was trembling like a leaf and my heart was pounding in my chest. All the time that I rushed to safety I wondered about Jack. That was a brave thing that he had done. Was he able to outrun the animal? I shivered again as I thought about him. There was nothing at all that I could do.

I slowed my steps and began to creep as quietly as I could toward the nest and the family. I felt chilled right to the bones but I wasn't sure if it was from the cold or the fright. I shivered again, aching for the warm bodies of my brother and sisters.

One thing I knew for sure. I had had my fill of night. Father and Mother were quite right. It was dangerous!

Chapter Nine

Storm

The day had started out sunny and bright. Pepe and I had fed until we were full enough that the hunger pangs were quieted but not so full that it would interfere with our running. We wanted to be at our best for the games.

Sandy was still annoying us and he was always there when we played. I had finally decided that the only way to make him smarten up was to see that he was 'it' a good portion of the time. I talked to all of the other fellows about it and it was decided that the next time we played, Sandy would be tagged time after time. We figured that with a concerted effort we could keep him running on a regular basis.

I would be the first 'it.' I simply would be slow in calling 'not it' when we began the game.

It worked just fine. I pretended to be studying the distant hills again and the other fellas all quickly hollered 'not it.' Of course Sandy yelled it before anyone else.

As the game began, I took my time looking

around the circle of fellas as though trying to decide just who to chase. Sandy began his usual taunting.

"You can't catch me. You can't catch me. Yah-h, yah-h, ya ya yah-h. You're slow as a turtle. Yah-h, yah-h ya ya yah-h."

I was getting awfully tired of Sandy.

Looking in the direction of Pepe, I made a sudden dash for Sandy. I caught him completely off guard and he took only two jumps when I tagged him.

He stood there in the middle of a 'yah-h' and began to flush a rosy red color. Then he realized that we were all waiting for him to chase someone so he started off after little Louis, the slowest one of us. At least you couldn't accuse Sandy of being dull.

He caught Louis without too much trouble. The agreement now was that one of us faster fellas would let Louis catch us right away. Louis picked Pepe. Pepe put on a little show, dancing around and making some faces like Sandy often did. Then he turned to run and pretended to trip and Louis caught him right off. Pepe then looked for a victim, studying out who to chase. Without too much hesitation, he started for Sandy. Sandy was caught off guard again. He started to run but didn't get far before he was tagged.

Sandy picked on Louis again. I guess he was afraid that he might not be able to catch anyone else. Louis tagged me and then, holding his side as though he had a sudden 'stitch,' he left the game to sit out on the sidelines.

The game went on. Now when Sandy was tagged he didn't have Louis to chase. He chose Emile, the next slowest of the bunch. This was repeated as one after the other of the fellas dropped out of the game to sit on the sidelines and watch. I held my breath.

I was sure that Sandy would catch on and join the fellas watching instead of taking part. But he didn't.

At last there was only Sandy, Pepe and me left.

Pepe and I really led him on a good round of chases. Just as soon as he would tag one of us we'd tag the other, who had had time to catch his breath, and then he would take off after Sandy. Sandy never did get much time for a break.

It was the most fun game of tag I had ever played. We sure took all of the 'yah-h, yah-h' out of Sandy. His tongue was practically dragging and his sides were heaving. We would have kept right on until he dropped I guess, but we heard a cry from the nearest sentry and we all froze in our tracks waiting for the next signal or the right to go on with the playing.

The second signal came and we all made a quick dash for home. As I ran I noticed the dark shadow of a hawk pass overhead. I hated the bird for breaking up our game and spoiling our fun. Someone should do something to stop him. Surely there was some way to outsmart him.

I ducked into the entrance passage and joined other members of the family. As they came in, one by one, Mother waited at the door, mentally ticking off each name. Louisa was the last, and latest. By then I could see the worry in Mother's eyes. But Louisa was really too plump to be able to run very fast. I knew that Mother was concerned about her weight but she didn't say so. Just moved over close to her and began to plant kisses on her cheeks and forehead. Louisa was trembling. Nothing was said, but I wondered if she had been given a real scare and if that hawk had nearly gotten her. It made me hate the hawk even more.

By the time the 'all clear' signal was given and we returned outside, the day had changed. The sun was no longer shining. Dark clouds rolled across the sky. Thunder rolled in the distance and lightning flashed.

I knew that it wouldn't be long until those clouds would be returning some of the moisture that they had gathered up from the earth. I was hungry. I hadn't eaten enough that morning and with the vigorous game of tag that we had played, I had worked that all off.

I hurried off to grab all I could before the storm began to splash all around me.

I didn't get to eat much. Soon large drops of rain began to spatter down all around me. I waited as long as I dared and then scurried off for home. I did hope that the rain didn't last long. I knew that the food supply in the storage rooms was considered 'for emergency use only' in the summer months and I was sure that Father would not consider playing tag instead of eating properly, an emergency.

Some of the family members were still gathered near the entrance when I came in. Mother scolded me about my wetness, then began to dry me off. I knew that she was there taking count of her offspring as they came in. Even Louisa had beaten me. She had gone on down to bed.

Sue Mary was there. For some reason I will never understand, she had a fascination with rain storms. I guess it was the booming thunder and the flashing lightning that interested her. She watched the storms as often as Mother would allow her to.

I stopped beside her for a few minutes and together we watched the storm as it raged outside. It was rather fascinating. Still, I hoped that it would soon pass over and we would be able to go back to feeding.

"I saw you playing tag," whispered Sue Mary.

I grinned. "Boy, did we have fun."

"It was quite obvious what you were doing," she went on, and then giggled.

"You know," I said in wonder, "I don't think that Sandy even caught on. He was so tired he could hardly wobble—yet he still didn't catch on."

"He will," said Sue Mary and her voice was more serious now. "And when he does, he'll be mad at someone."

"Who?" I quickly cut in.

"Whoever he thinks came up with the idea, I expect," said Sue Mary.

That was me. I had a feeling that Sue Mary also had guessed that it was me.

"Aw," I said in mock bravery, "I'm not afraid of him. He's all talk."

"He's big, Flick. And he won't fight fair, you know that."

It was true. Sue Mary had Sandy figured out pretty good. I was surprised that, as a girl, she knew so much about him.

"Be careful," she whispered.

The thunder and lightning seemed to have moved off into the distance. I was all ready to go back out to eat but the rain didn't stop. It just kept coming down, coming down, in steady sheets of cold water. I wondered how the clouds could hold so much of it. I soon tired of watching it and went off down to bed for a nap.

When I got up again my stomach was complaining. I crept up the passageway to look out at the day. Surely the rain had stopped by now.

But it hadn't. It was still falling just as steadily. One certainly couldn't feed in that.

I went back to bed grumbling. I had the feeling that my stomach wasn't going to let me get much sleep.

After a while I tried again—then again—but each time that I checked, the rain was still falling.

I thought that I would starve to death before I was able to get back to feeding. Father didn't seem to think so. He said, "We can wait to eat. The food in the storage room must be kept for emergencies only."

I was sure that this was a real emergency.

Finally I could stand it no longer. I sneaked from the den and went out to eat.

Everywhere I went there was water. My feet were wet before I took three steps and they soon were so cold I could hardly stand it.

My fur got wet too. The heavy rain continued to beat down upon my back, soaking me right through to the skin. I hated the water but my hunger caused me to try to ignore it.

Feeding was difficult. Every blade of grass that I plucked was also covered with water. I didn't mind the freshness and the sweetness of the moisture, but when I tugged at the grass a shower of cold wetness was dumped on my head and shoulders. It was not fun feeding in the rain.

I hurried as quickly as I could, grabbing mouthfuls and chewing them quickly so that I could reach for another. At last my hunger was assuaged enough for me to think that I could wait out the storm. I hurried toward home thinking now of the warmth that the snuggling family in the cozy nest

would provide me.

Mother met me at the entrance to the nest. I guess she heard me coming down the passageway as I hadn't tried to be quiet.

"Where have you been?" she asked me with sharpness in her voice.

"Out! Eating. I was starved."

"There was plenty of time to eat before the storm came," she reminded me.

"I know but I was—was—busy." I finished lamely.

I could feel Mother's eyes probing me again.

"Busy?" she said.

"Yeah, I—." I stopped and shivered.

"You're soaked to the bone," she observed. "You'll catch your death of cold."

"I'll soon warm up when I get to bed," I informed her, making an attempt to brush on past and head for the bed.

"Oh, no you don't," said Mother taking a firm stand. "You aren't crawling into bed soaked like that. You'll get the bedding and your family all soaked, too."

I looked down at myself. I supposed she was right, but I was freezing. How would I ever warm up if I couldn't go to bed? Where would I sleep?

Mother told me. "You can sleep in the empty storage room," she said and I shivered again just at the thought. There was not even bedding in the empty storage room.

"Come," she said. "I'll dry you off the best I can."

So saying, she led me to the empty room and began to groom the water from my fur. There wasn't too much that she could do. When she had finished I was still wet and cold.

When she left, I curled up the best I could and

tried to go to sleep in spite of my shaking body. Mother was soon back. She had brought me some bedding from the nest.

"This might help some," she said as she tucked it about me. "Try to get some sleep."

I tried, but it sure was difficult to do. I was shivering so much that my whole body shook. I wondered just which was worse—being cold or being hungry.

Chapter Ten

Rained Out

I had never seen so much rain in all my life. I thought that the sky must surely be falling down. The clouds kept pouring down so much water.

Everyone was getting hungry. Even Father. But it was just too miserable for us to go out to eat. Finally even Father conceded that it was indeed an emergency. He rationed out some of the food from the storage room. It really wasn't enough to satisfy our deep hunger but at least it took the edge off of it.

To make life more bearable, we tried to sleep all we could. That worked for awhile, but soon sleep, too, eluded us. We were hungry, restless and miserable and though Mother tried hard to keep us entertained, even she was about to give up. Little squabbles kept breaking out over petty little differences and it was terribly hard on everyone's nerves.

Father checked frequently just to see what was going on outside. Family members checked frequently, too, because we were anxious to get turned loose again, not that we were watching for possible danger.

Our home had been built with safety in mind. The mound around the edge was made to keep out the water when rain began to cover the ground around us. But even with that safety factor, if the water level around us got too high, we would be in trouble.

Father watched as the rain formed huge puddles, he watched more carefully as the puddles joined together to form big pools. Soon our whole area was beginning to look like a lake with the edges of prairie dog homes sticking up through the water.

Father checked again and came back with a worried look on his face. Mother looked at him and he nodded his head solemnly without saying a word. Then the two of them began to move and pack dirt solidly into the entrance of the tunnel.

At first I couldn't figure out what they were doing. I guess my eyes must have held my questions for Father stopped long enough to explain.

"We're going to seal off this entrance against the rain. The back entrance is higher. If we need to get out, we'll use it.

We had never been allowed to use the back entrance before. In fact, it was always partially closed off. I welcomed the chance to see just where the back entrance took us. For a moment I half hoped that we would need it.

Father and Mother worked steadily in sealing off the passageway. They were careful to place the dirt on the far side of some of the storage rooms. They knew that we would likely need the food before the rain abated.

Once they had the tunnel sealed as securely as they could, Father busied himself opening up the back entrance. He didn't want to take any chances if we needed the back door as an escape.

"If it should happen that the front dam does not hold," he warned us all, "the minute that you see it begin to break, you must all rush out the back entrance as quickly as you can. Don't stop to look, do you hear? You just run. The minute you hear my signal, you run."

We all understood.

"Just hope it isn't in the middle of the night," I heard Mother say under her breath.

The very words made me shiver. I had never shared with any of them my experiences with the night creatures, but I sure wasn't anxious to go out into the night again.

We youngsters curled up together and slept as usual. I guess Mother and Father spent the entire night keeping watch on the earthen dam that they had constructed to hold the water out. I don't know if they watched together or took turns but it seemed that neither of them got much sleep.

The dam did hold for the night. My stomach was beginning to gnaw at me, trying to get its message through to me that it was time to get up and look for breakfast. Sleep was still refusing to let me go, when I heard Father's alarm. It sounded not once, but twice, one right after the other. All five of us were instantly on our feet and moving before we were really awake. I just hoped that I was going in the right direction.

I had looked forward to using the back entrance, but now, in my haste, I didn't even take notice of it. I just ran—and as I was the last one in line, I saw the dam on the front entrance break just behind me and the water came whishing up against my hind legs. That frightened me even more and I shoved hard against the retreating form of Annabelle who was just ahead of me.

I was sure that we'd never make it. The cold water was already washing over me. I struggled to stay on my feet and ran desperately. My coat was already soaked and I hated the feel of water closing in around my head. I knew that Annabelle was running through water as well and I hoped that she would be smart enough not to take a breath while she was running. If she did, we'd both be in real trouble.

Just as I thought that I couldn't possibly hold my breath or my lungs would burst, my head broke through the water and I could breathe again. In a few more steps I had cleared the back entrance and was out on the open prairie. At least it *had* been the open prairie. Now it looked far more like the open sea.

Water was everywhere. I couldn't believe my eyes.

I don't suppose it was deep but it lay all around us. Here and there the mound that marked a prairie dog home still showed, but water covered where I knew many neighbors' homes to be. There was nothing to show that they had ever been there. I looked around, wondering what had happened to all our friends.

It was the first that I noticed the crowd clustered around on the higher ground and rock outcroppings. Here and there were shivering families, clinging together for some kind of warmth and security. A few of the younger children whimpered but were immediately hushed. No one wanted any noise that would alert our enemies to our predicament.

We were a silent, cold, bedraggled-looking lot. I could see that I wasn't the only one who had had to swim my way to the top. I knew that the others had hated it every bit as much as I had.

It was still raining. The sky was overcast and looked as if it would keep on raining forever. I shivered again at the thought.

I found my eyes scanning the crowds to see if I could spot any of my friends. One by one I found several of them but I didn't spy Pepe. I was beginning to be really concerned when Sue Mary gave me a jab with a sharp little elbow.

"Look over there, on that shelf of rock. See that family huddled there. Is that Pepe's sister?"

I followed her eye. It was. I was sure of that. But I still couldn't see Pepe. I was really worried now. And then the family members shifted around and Pepe moved to the fore. I was so relieved to see him that I wanted to shout a greeting, but I knew better than to do that. I didn't even dare to wave.

There was nothing to do. No place to go. No place to get in out of the rain. We just had to stand right there and let it run down our backs and drip off our noses. I had never been so miserable in my life.

We couldn't even feed. All of our roots and grasses were under water. I wondered what we would ever do for dinner.

It was late in the afternoon before the rain ceased. I hadn't realized that there had been one blessing in the steady downpour. The hawks had not been flying. As soon as the rain stopped and the clouds rolled away, the sun came out and they were back in the sky again.

We were all in a panic. We were helpless before them now. There was no place to run to hide.

As many as possible pressed under the rock overhangs. Others pushed into sagebrush or grass clumps—anywhere where they could find some kind of cover.

It seemed almost miraculous that no lives were lost throughout the day. As the sun dipped into the west and the hawks went to roost for the night I breathed a sigh of relief. Our family was still intact.

And then I thought of the night creatures and my exuberance seeped away from me. We now faced the night and I knew a little about the dangers of the nighttime. I was scared.

The moon came out, big and bright. I wasn't sure if that would help or hinder our cause. I knew that I needed it to see but I also knew that the night creatures seemed to be able to see too well with its help.

It was then that I spied Jack. I was relieved to see him as it was the first that I had seen him since the night I had slipped from the nest and he had diverted the coyote so that I could make it safely home.

I guess my relief showed in my face but I didn't dare say too much with my family members around. I knew that Mother or Father would be asking questions if I hinted at anything concerning that night.

Jack looked at me and I caught his wink. Then he turned to my father.

"You folks need some help?" he asked, sincerely enough.

"I guess we need about all the help we can get," my father admitted, "though I'm not sure how you'd be able to help us."

"Well, I can't give you back your home, that's for sure," said Jack, "but I do happen to know where there is a place that is warm and dry, even though it isn't quite what you have been used to."

Father nodded solemnly. I knew that he was

anxious to get the family in out of the open.

"Interested?" asked Jack.

"Certainly," responded Father, then added politely, "thank you."

"No problem," said Jack, and he began to lead the way to somewhere that I had never been before.

Jack caught himself going a bit too fast for us every now and then and he'd have to slow down again to accommodate us. It turned out to be much further away than any of us had expected and it seemed that it was all up hill.

When we go there it was just as Jack had said. The place was warm and dry and sheltered from the night creatures, too.

It was a hollow spot under a fallen tree on the lea side of the hill looking down over the prairie. It looked snug and warm and I knew that my folks were thankful for it. Still, Mother couldn't help but wrinkle up her nose as she entered. It seemed that the place had previously been occupied by a woodchuck family and Mother did not care much for the smell of the place.

However, we didn't turn it down. We thanked Jack and one by one the family members shuffled over the high door sill and began to snuggle up with one another for warmth and safety.

I was the last one so I got to whisper a few words to Jack.

"Glad you're okay," I said in a soft voice so that I wouldn't be heard by family members. "I was worried about you."

"Ha-a!" he answered in a swaggering tone. "No need to worry. It'll be the day when those two coyotes can outrun me." Then he called a goodnight and was off.

The home might not have been what we were used to, but we sure were glad to have it. We snuggled close together and tried to forget our empty stomachs in our thankfulness to have a roof over our heads. I guess we all slept. I know that I did.

When I awakened again, the sun was shining. It was strange to wake up to sunshine. I was used to waking up way down in our underground nest where darkness enveloped you day or night. Here we were with the sun streaming in upon us, warming our backs through the leaves of the tangled branches.

We all began to stir and even before any of us had our eyes open I heard Louisa say, "I'm hungry."

I could have echoed the words. I was starving.

We found when we left the borrowed nest that Jack had done us another favor. We were above the water level. Here there was food for foraging. It didn't take us long to decide that eating was a very good idea.

Father and Mother took the first shift as sentries. We youngsters lost no time in beginning to see what we could find to eat. The food was quite plentiful and we were so hungry that we dove right in.

After we had eaten enough to feel more comfortable, Frisk volunteered to take a shift as sentry and let Father and Mother eat. Father knew that none of us had ever served as sentry before, so he suggested that Mother eat while he stayed on duty with Frisk. Then it was to be my turn. Mother and I would watch while Father ate.

It was fun to be sentry. My only disappointment

was that there was never any reason to give the distress signal. I was rather anxious to try mine. I had never had opportunity to use it.

One by one we all had a turn, with either Father or Mother pairing off with each one of us.

All day long Father kept his eye on the prairie land below us. I knew that both he and Mother were anxious to get back to our own home. It still didn't look very hopeful to me and besides I really liked the home we were presently occupying. You could see so much more right from your own bed-room.

We were into the third day before Father decided that things looked dry enough down below to get on with the clean-up chores. We all knew that there was a big job ahead of us. I had the feeling that we were now considered old enough to share the load.

We started back down the slope, Father's eye ever on the sky and Mother's roaming back and forth over the land all around us. Seeing their watchfulness made me feel all excited and tingly inside. I knew that danger lurked all around us.

When we got home we found a nightmare. All around us neighbors were frantically trying to dig out and repair their homes. Several families were in mourning. The storm and the days that followed with no protection from their enemies resulted in a number of deaths in neighborhood families. I shuddered as I thought about it and was even more thankful for Jack. I guess Father and Mother were, too, for I heard Mother say to Father, "We must remember to do something nice for that kind Jack Rabbit. It was so nice of him to think of us."

"It was," responded Father. Then he added slowly, "And curious, too."

"Curious?" said Mother.

"Yes. Why did he seek us out, do you suppose? There were any number of families in the same fix. Why did he seem to be looking for us?"

"Why I don't know," said Mother. "I hadn't even thought about it, but it does seem that way, doesn't it?"

Then Mother's eyes turned directly on me. I felt that she was looking right through me. I couldn't help but squirm but I hoped with all of my heart that she didn't catch the squirming.

"Would you know anything about it, Flick?" Mother asked me.

"Me? Why should I? I've seen him around lots of times. He's always hopping here or there. Haven't you seen him?"

I was hoping that my evasiveness would throw them off, but I'm not sure that it worked. I still felt Mother's eyes on me.

We all set to work on our house. It had to be all dug out again. It still felt a bit damp in spots but Father assured us that it would soon dry out. Mother and the girls managed to find some dry bedding someplace and they began to make our bed again. Our emergency food supply was the biggest concern. It was hard enough to find grasses to fill our hungry tummies, let alone extra for storing. I had the feeling that it would be some time until we felt safe and contented again.

Chapter Eleven

Boomerang

We didn't do much playing over the next few days. We were still too busy helping our families finish the clean-up and the foraging for a new supply of stored food. It took all of us working together to get even a small emergency supply gathered. We had another problem, too. Our enemies all knew our predicament and they hovered nearby, ready to take quick advantage of our situation.

The sentries were busier than ever. In fact, there were additional sentries posted for each shift and often during the day the warning signal was given. It was usually hawks and I learned to hate them for keeping us in constant fear.

It was hard to work and watch. But we soon learned to do it. All of us were edgy and tempers were short.

I remember seeing some real disputes. It seemed that we all were in bad need of food and the grass and roots were limited because of the flooding. To make matters worse, the hawks had everyone's nerves rubbed raw. That meant that any little thing could set off a quarrel.

If a fight broke out close to where we fed or worked, the girls always ran for home with their eyes half shut and their faces screwed up in horror. I laughed. What did they have to fear? As long as they minded their own business no one was going to touch them. I enjoyed watching the disagreements myself.

At long last Father decided that we could take a break or two along with the food gathering and we went back to a game of tag.

It was the first that we had played together for some time so it was a real treat to get back together. I supposed that everyone had forgotten about our last game. But I guess no one had.

I saw Louis look at me with a question in his eyes and I knew that he was wondering if we were going to play it the same way we had the last one. I nodded slightly and he passed the nod along to the other fellows.

I didn't start out being 'it.' I thought that was just too obvious. I had Sue Mary's words still nagging at the back of my mind.

Louis was first 'it.' He caught Frisk who caught me and I went right after Sandy. He didn't say anything at the time and I thought that he had completely forgotten the last game that we had played.

After Sandy was tagged, he caught Louis, who caught Pepe, who went after Sandy again. Sandy tagged Louis, who caught me and I again went after Sandy.

Sandy immediately informed us that he was dropping out. The game proceeded as normal from then on. I guessed that maybe Sandy was getting a bit suspicious. None of the other fellas dropped out as they had the previous game.

I didn't think too much of the whole thing. We didn't really have too much time to play before we were called to go back to work anyway and we parted company and went on with our tasks.

I was busy gathering roots a little way from the rest of the family members when I heard a slight stirring behind me.

I looked up expecting to see Jack. He had come in close enough to say "Hi' a number of times recently when he had spotted me a bit apart from the family. In fact that was one reason why I tried to put a bit of distance between myself and the other family members.

To my surprise it wasn't Jack. It was Sandy. I felt some disappointment but I paid little attention to him and went on filling my mouth with roots to haul back to the storage rooms.

I should have been watching him more carefully.

Before I knew what was happening, a sharp strike against my left jaw sent me reeling. I jerked myself around and faced Sandy head-on.

"So you think you're some kind of smart guy, huh, Kersworth?" he asked me.

I said nothing, just blinked. My jaw was hurting something awful.

Before I could even move, he struck me again.

"Come on if you're so smart," he said. "Let's see you stand on your own four feet."

I knew that Sandy was way too big for me to handle. I knew that he was rough and mean as well and that didn't make me feel any better about facing him. I didn't back down but I didn't rush him either.

"Come on if you're so tough," he hurled at me. "Let's see you show it."

"What're you talking about?" I finally managed through my clenched teeth. I was afraid to open my mouth for fear the teeth would all fall out.

"What am I talking about? You know very well. You think I'm so dense I wouldn't catch on?"

I didn't want to answer that.

"Well, I caught on," he said, anger making the fur along his neck stand out. "I know you rigged the game."

"Me?" I said innocently. "What do you mean— me?"

"Don't try to be cool, Kersworth. I know it was you. Nobody else thinks in such a dumb way. You did it and you know it."

"Me?" I said again, but even I knew that I wasn't very convincing.

By now I had dropped all of the grass that I had gathered. I had worked hard to forage for the supplies. Now it lay scattered all about me. It made me mad. Without even thinking of the consequences I threw myself at Sandy.

I should have known better. With one strong blow he knocked me right off my feet. Now my other cheek was hurting. I wondered if I'd have any teeth left at all.

I pulled myself to my feet, shaking my head to clear the fog and rushed him again.

It was the same as before. I was knocked back down before I could even land a blow.

Sandy laughed—a cruel, weird laugh. "Come on, dumbhead," he said. "I see you're not so smart after all."

I was beginning to agree with Sandy.

"Come on," he said again, squaring himself for my rush. "Come on. Try me again."

I did. But I shouldn't have. I was just so mad that I couldn't stop myself. Besides I had to live with myself and I didn't want to admit that I was a coward.

The results were the same. Sandy sent me flying. This time he lifted me right off my feet and sent me hurtling through the air. I landed on my side with a 'thump,' and it knocked the wind right out of me.

It was through my dazed condition that I heard a sharp little voice, "Stop that, you big bully! Stop that, do you hear me?" and I looked up to see Sue Mary hurl herself at big old Sandy and begin to pound on his huge body with tiny little fists.

I guess it caught Sandy totally by surprise for a minute. He just stood and blinked and let Sue Mary beat on him. Then he reached out and roughly pushed her, knocking her right down.

"You mean the sissy has to have a girl fight his battle?" he hissed. Then added menacingly, "You'd better stay out of this if you know what's good for you, kid. I'm not done yet."

And he came at me again.

Sue Mary was crying now but she jumped back onto her feet and began to pound on Sandy again. It didn't stop him. It didn't even slow him down. He was determined to finish the job he had started on me and he brushed Sue Mary roughly aside and came at me.

"Sue Mary stay out of it," I called to her. "You'll get hurt."

"Yeah," hissed Sandy. "Listen to your brave, strong, big brother." Then he turned to me. "So who's going to protect your little sister, Wimp? You?

Not likely. In fact I'm gonna knock that one lonely brain of yours right out of your little skull," and he moved forward to do just that.

"I wouldn't," I heard a voice say and I blinked to see what was happening now. I still hadn't been able to catch my breath enough to right myself. I was struggling hard to get my feet under me before Sandy reached me again. At least then I could run if nothing else.

It was Louisa who blocked the path between Sandy and me.

Now if Sue Mary was smaller than most of the youngsters our age, Louisa made up for it. She was definitely bigger than any of the other girls and also bigger than most of the other fellas. In fact, she and Sandy were in a class all by themselves.

I started to warn Louisa to stay back, that Sandy was tough and that he wouldn't think twice about hitting a girl, but I still didn't have breath to talk and then Louisa leaped forward and lashed out at Sandy. I had never seen her move so fast in all of her life. I couldn't believe my eyes.

"Good going," came a little voice and I saw Sue Mary leap to her feet at Louisa's side.

That slowed Sandy down some.

"Two women," he hissed. "The nerd needs two women to protect him."

"No, not women," said Louisa as she braced herself for another attack. "Sisters! Just sisters. And you'd better not lay a hand on my brother again or you'll have to answer to me. Do you hear me? Wimp."

I guess Sandy did. At any rate he didn't say another word, just mumbled some threats under his breath and turned and left us.

I hardly knew what to say to the girls. I guess I really didn't have to say much of anything. They must have known how grateful I was.

They lifted me and began cleaning me up before Mother would see me.

I was worried about facing Mother. I knew that she wouldn't dismiss this too easily. I decided I'd better get some stories worked out with the girls.

"What're you gonna tell Mother?" I asked them.

They exchanged looks. It was Louisa who finally spoke.

"We won't say anything unless we are asked," she said matter-of-factly. "If we are asked, we'll suggest she ask you."

That was a real relief. Still, I didn't know if the girls would really be able to put Mother off if she decided to start asking questions.

"Come on. Let's get home," said Louisa.

"I can't," I responded rubbing my injured jaw. "I need to gather food for the storage room."

"We'll help," offered Sue Mary and both girls began to help me gather up the grass that had been scattered in the scuffle.

"Do you think he'll bother Flick again?" Sue Mary asked Louisa.

"Naw," said Louisa with confidence. "He's a sissy under all that boasting. He's scared to try."

I did hope that Louisa was right but I wasn't quite as confident as the seemed to be. I decided that, for the time being, I would stay a little closer to my family members.

The girls helped me home with the food supply and we deposited it in the storage room. It made a bigger pile than I could have gathered on my own and when Father checked it later, he gave me a nice compliment on a job well done. I didn't tell him that I'd had help. I was afraid that I might have to explain why the girls had helped me.

No one noticed my swollen jaws or scratched sides that night. I snuggled up and went to bed earlier than usual. I lay a bit apart hoping that I wouldn't be bumped as people turned over in the night. It could hurt pretty bad if they bumped up against my sore ribs or my aching jaws.

Somehow I made it through the night but, boy, did I dread the thought of facing Father and Mother the next morning.

Chapter Twelve

Sisters

Mother was the first to notice me. I knew that she would be. I heard her little gasp and Father's head came up. I could feel his eyes on me, too.

"What happened?" she asked.

I had spent a good share of the night trying to think of a way to evade that question. I hadn't come up with anything. Now that it was asked I knew that she expected an answer.

I had also spent a great deal of time trying to think of an answer. I had thought of several—but none of them seemed very good. At last I had decided that I'd probably just have to make one up.

I hated to call it lying—it was more like stretching the truth. Before, I had always tried to get by with *evading* the truth. I just hadn't said all that should have been said to give Mother the facts that she wanted. Now, I knew that I couldn't even start with the facts. It would just mean more questions. So I decided that I'd just have to make up the story as I went along.

"I bumped myself," I muttered, barely moving my

swollen jaws. Boy, did it hurt to talk.

"Bumped yourself?" said Mother in an incredulous tone. I could tell that she didn't believe my story.

I wished that I had picked the one about being chased by a coyote. I decided to combine the two.

"Yeah, I was gathering food for the storage shed—," I thought that added a nice touch. My folks were bound to have more sympathy knowing that I was 'on duty' at the time of the mishap.

"I was gathering food," I started again, "and this here coyote came along and—."

Mother stopped me with a sharp look at Father. "I didn't hear any alarm yesterday," she said quickly.

"Oh—well—there wasn't an alarm, you see—."

"You saw a coyote—right in town and didn't send out an alarm?"

Mother couldn't believe that I could be that dense.

"Well—er—well, there wasn't time," I quickly put in—and he wasn't really that close. I just saw him and I was running to tell the sentry—only I was watching him to see which way he was going to go and I ran right into this rock and bumped my jaw."

I had finished my story in haste and confusion. I really wasn't very good at lying. I hoped with all of my heart that Mother would buy the story. She didn't. I could tell that by her eyes. Maybe the one I had thought of about the rock falling on me would have been better. I wished that I could use it instead, and even thought about trying but it seemed a little late now.

"You bumped right into a rock?" Mother repeated.

I nodded. It hurt too much to talk. It hurt to nod, too.

"Who was holding the rock?" asked Mother.

"Well—," I didn't have much time to think. Pepe was the first name that came to my mind, but I didn't want to get Pepe involved in the story. He would tell the truth if asked—and Mother was likely to ask. He hadn't been anywhere around at the time. Then I thought of Sandy. Whether he would tell the truth or not was debatable. I was quite sure that Mother would doubt him, no matter what he said.

"Sandy," I muttered. "Sandy was holding it."

The girls had been silent the whole time but I saw the looks on their faces. They couldn't believe that I would stray so far from the truth.

"Sandy—," I began, but Mother cut in.

"Sandy swung it?" she said and before I took time to think I said, "Yeah," and then I caught myself.

Mother—in her own way, had just gotten me to admit that I'd been fighting with Sandy. Oh, there hadn't been any rock involved, but that was incidental. I broke away from the truth again and started to sputter and explain.

"No, he wasn't holding it. He didn't swing it, either. He was just standing by it and he didn't move and when I hit the rock it didn't even budge because Sandy was right there against it and he's big and—."

"So Sandy was there with the coyote, too?"

"Well he—he was—yeah." I finished lamely.

"And he didn't send the alarm, either."

"He didn't see it. He had his back to it."

That sounded pretty good.

"He was too busy swinging the rock." This came from Father.

"Yeah," I cut in quickly and then realized that I'd

been fooled again. I began to blush and to stammer.

"No—no. He wasn't swinging the rock. Just leaning on the rock. He was leaning or—or something."

"Flick," said Mother sternly, "you don't make a very good storyteller."

She didn't say liar. Mother hated lies. I knew that it hurt her deeply that one of her offspring would be telling anything but the truth.

She looked at me—long and hard, like she was trying to look past my swollen face into my very soul.

Then she sighed deeply and nodded her head slightly. "Let's take a look at it," she said.

I followed her nod. I knew that she would take me to one of the empty storage rooms where there was more room to work. I moved forward and then my breath caught in a little sob. I had forgotten about my sore ribs. I remembered them now. Boy, did they hurt!

"So you bumped more than your jaw," observed Mother.

"Yeah," I said, and it was almost a whimper.

I followed Mother—slowly. It hurt so much to move that I just eased myself along.

"I would suggest that you stay very near to the entrance today," Mother said. "If an enemy comes, you won't be able to do much running."

Mother was right about that. I nodded. The nodding hurt, too.

Mother examined me carefully, kindly, but even her touch hurt.

"I don't think anything is broken," she said at last, "just bruised. But you will be pretty sore for several days."

I nodded slowly.

"I don't believe your story—you know that, Flick."

I started to nod slowly again and then realized that I should be protecting myself.

"But I was," I insisted. "I did."

"No Flick," said Mother while shaking her head sadly. "The story doesn't even make sense."

"It does." I blurted. "It—."

"You keep tripping yourself up. You change the story every time you open your mouth," she reminded me.

"But I—," I began.

"Let's not say anymore," cut in Mother. "Not until you decide to tell me the whole truth about the matter."

She looked at me coolly. "And about a few other matters as well," she said with a weary sigh.

I did as Mother said and stayed close to home to feed that day. I couldn't eat very well anyway. It hurt too much to chew, so I finally just gave up and slowly dragged myself back to the nest.

Louisa soon joined me. I was very grateful for Louisa. She had saved my hide and I knew it. She didn't scold, but I knew that she was terribly disappointed in me. Louisa, like Mother, thought that the truth should be told at all cost.

Sue Mary came in next. She curled up beside me and gently soothed my hurting jaw.

Then she surprised me.

"Why didn't you tell it like it was, Flick?" she asked me. "Mother will find out anyway. Do you know where she is right now? She's visiting Sandy's place."

I jerked my head up, making me 'oh-h-h' with pain.

"Why'd she go do that?" I protested.

"Because she wants the truth," said Sue Mary flatly.

We were quiet for a few minutes, then she went on softly. "It would have been so much better if you'd told her the whole truth to begin with," she said. "Trying to make up some fancy story didn't fool Mother for a minute. She would have understood about your fight with Sandy. Young fellas often get into tangles about one thing or another. Mother could have forgiven that."

The implication was that Mother wouldn't forgive my lies.

I wanted to protest, but deep down I saw that Sue Mary's reasoning made sense. Why had I been afraid to tell the truth? Why had I felt that lying was a way out? I had no answer to any of my questions.

"Now, try to sleep," Sue Mary soothed, without further comment.

I would have been only too glad to sleep—if I could have. My conscience was about as raw and sore as my jaw.

I didn't sleep much—but I was happy for the company of my sisters.

In the days that followed my jaw and my side gradually improved. I lost some weight in the process. I just wasn't able to eat like I usually did. I sure would be glad when things were back to normal again.

Mother hadn't said anything after her trip to Sandy's. I have no idea what he told her. I couldn't see him admitting that he had attacked me. I couldn't see him admitting that the girls had fought him off, either. Sandy's ego wouldn't allow him to admit that.

The days generally settled down again. Things did get back to normal and I was even able to make up some of the lost weight again. It was a real relief. I was foolish enough to think that the whole incident was behind us. And then Annabelle got sick.

If I had been asked to name my family members in the order of preference, I suppose I would have named Annabelle last. I mean, it wasn't that I didn't care for her or anything, it was just that she and I had very little in common and we never played together or shared secrets or anything, but when she took sick suddenly, mysteriously, I was worried. I mean, I was really worried.

Mother was beside herself with concern. If she had had some idea of the cause of Annabelle's illness she would have had a better idea what to do about it, but not knowing, she had no idea how to treat her.

Annabelle was really sick, too. We all knew that. I was afraid that she was going to die—and I knew that Mother was afraid of that, too.

We all walked around on tiptoe. No one spoke except in whispers. We all tried to think of things we could do—ways we could help, but there really wasn't much.

The girls found extra bedding and placed it in the empty storage room and the family—all but Annabelle and Mother slept there so that we wouldn't disturb her. Daily we carried her fresh bedding and discarded the old. That was about all that we could do for her comfort.

Her fever stayed high and her breathing ragged and I was scared to death. I was afraid that my

sister was ill to punish me for my awful lying. It
was the first that I had really admitted to myself
that I had been lying. Before, I always used words
like 'stretching the truth,' or 'telling a story' or even
'little white lies,' but now I finally admitted to
myself that I had done far more than that. I had
lied. Out-and-out lied to try to protect myself. And
the funny part of it was the incident hadn't even
been my fault. Sandy had jumped *me*.

I was just on the verge of confessing the whole
thing when Annabelle's fever broke. What a relief it
was to us all. Especially to Mother. And I guess to
me, too. Now I wouldn't have to unburden myself
after all. I busied myself, along with the rest of the
family, in finding Annabelle special treats of tender
roots and grasses. I even went back to my old spot
to see if some of the extra-special roots had decided
to grow again. I found just one. It was so tempting
to just eat it myself but I took it to Annabelle. It
was sort of a peace offering for my own soul. I felt
that by giving it away I might somehow balance
the scales again—or maybe even tip them just a bit
in my favor.

Annabelle slowly improved. At last she was able
to be up and outside. The old bedding was taken
away and fresh, new bedding installed and the
family was able to move back to the nest again.

It was then that I noticed Mother. She was
almost as pale and as thin as Annabelle. I wished
with all of my heart that I could find just one more
special root. I would have shared that one with
Mother.

Chapter Thirteen

Danger

I hadn't seen Pepe for a number of days. With my injury and Annabelle's illness I hadn't been playing the community games much for several days. Now that I was feeling better and Annabelle was out of danger, I decided to look Pepe up.

I didn't need to go far. I found him sunning himself on a nearby rock and watching the young girls as they played skip rope. I noticed that Sue Mary was among the girls and also noticed that Pepe's eyes lingered mostly on her. I stood there, silently watching Pepe until he noticed me, grinned, blushed and called, "Hi."

"Won't you join me?" he asked good-naturedly, making room for me beside him on the rock. "I've found a new activity—and it's more fun than tag. It's called 'girl-watching.'"

Pepe laughed and I flopped down beside him.

I was about to tell him how foolish I thought his new game was when I noticed a certain girl in the group. She was new to me—and boy, was she cute.

"Who's that?" I asked Pepe.

He swung around to look at me as though surprised that I didn't know.

"That's Sassy."

"Sassy? Sassy who? I don't think I've ever seen her before. Did they just move in?"

"You've seen her before," said Pepe evenly. "She's just grown up a bit that's all. It's Sassy. Sandy's kid sister."

I couldn't believe my ears—nor my eyes. The tubby little sister of Sandy had suddenly become a very good-looking young lady. I shook my head. Good looking or not, I had no intention of getting mixed up with any sister of Sandy's.

"So what's so much fun about this?" I asked Pepe grumpily.

"Just watch," he said, "you'll see."

I settled down to watch. It didn't take me too long to really get to enjoy the game. I mean, some of those girls were getting pretty cute.

They changed their game after awhile and began to play some form of ball toss. It seemed to take a good deal of squealing, a measure of giggling and very little skill. They had fun though, and I was rather enjoying watching them, too.

They hadn't played for long when Sue Mary smacked the ball hard and it bounded right over Sassy's head. It bounced our way and I saw it as a good opportunity to sort of get involved—or at least noticed, if you know what I mean. I jumped down off the rock and headed for the ball just as she came to get it and we nearly collided in the process.

She flushed a pretty pink and lowered her head shyly and I grinned as I carefully and rather brashly handed her the ball. Our eyes met for just a second and I saw the twinkle in hers. I wondered if my eyes gave away my feelings also. And then she was gone again and I heaved a big sigh and stood there looking after her.

I guess I stood there for a long time, I don't know. The first thing that brought me back to attention was a call from Pepe.

"Hey, Flick. Flick! You gone and flipped or something?"

He laughed and I flushed somewhat and went back to join him on the rock.

We were silent for a long time and then Pepe spoke.

"Doesn't seem fair does it?"

"What doesn't?" I puzzled.

"That the cutest girl out there—in your eyes—is the sister of your enemy."

"What you talking about?" I asked angrily. "I don't have an enemy."

"Begging your pardon," said Pepe with a grin. "The way that Sandy has been talking lately, I was sure that he was your enemy."

That made my ears perk up.

"So what's the jerk been saying?" I asked.

"That he trimmed you. That you crawled. That he'll fix you even worse the next time."

"The nerd!" I said through clenched teeth.

"It's not true?" asked Pepe.

I squirmed. "He jumped me," I sputtered. "He jumped me when I wasn't even looking. You call that trimming a guy?"

Pepe didn't answer my question. He was very thoughtful and then he said slowly, "He's not the kind that you want for an enemy, Flick. If I were you I'd be careful. He's way bigger than you are and he fights mean. I wouldn't pick a fight with him if I were you."

"I didn't pick it."

"Let me put it another way," went on Pepe. "I'd avoid it. Fights only mean trouble."

"Aw," I said, "lots of fellas fight. I've seen dozens of them and they never amount to much."

"Oh, that's different," said Pepe waving it aside. "They're only little skirmishes when tempers are a little short. Boundary disputes or family rows. That's not like this Flick. Sandy is out to get you— unless, of course, you apologize."

"Me apologize? It was *him* that jumped *me,*" I almost shouted my indignity.

"Sure—he jumped you. But you provoked it with your game idea."

"Look," I reminded Pepe, "you were in on that game-plan, too."

"I know," said Pepe, avoiding my eyes. "I've already apologized."

I couldn't believe my ears.

"You what?"

"Face it, Flick. We have never been nice to Sandy. No wonder he acted like he did. We never included him in the games or tried to get along with him or anything. Can you imagine what it would be like to be left out all of the time? We never gave him a chance to be anything else than what we made him to be."

The whole thing sounded crazy to me. I wanted to hotly deny everything that Pepe was saying, but I knew that there was a grain of truth in it. I didn't say anything. At least not until I'd had time to simmer down some.

"So—?"

"So what?" asked Pepe.

"What did he do? Say?"

Pepe's eyes were back on Sue Mary. "Who?" he asked absently.

"Oh, come on, Pepe," I said in disgust. "We were talking about Sandy, remember? You said you'd apologized. What did he say?"

"Oh," said Pepe, his eyes still not leaving Sue Mary. "He said 'Sure.' "

"Sure what?" I prompted.

"Sure he'd forget the whole thing. We're friends."

Now I had really heard everything.

Instead of making me feel good, it made me mad.

"So," I said. "Guess you don't need me hanging around, huh? Now that you've got your good friend Sandy."

I slid off the rock and started away from Pepe.

"Aw, come on Flick," he called after me. "Don't be a nerd."

I just kept right on walking and Pepe didn't try to stop me again.

I had a long time by myself to think over what Pepe had said. Maybe it did make some sense There was no use making enemies right in town. We had enough enemies without that.

I was busy mulling it all over in my mind when I heard a strange noise. It sounded like distant thunder and then it seemed to be getting closer and closer. I stood up on my hind legs and tried to see what it might be but all that I saw was a very strange cloud off to the right.

I lowered myself and went back to feeding. It seemed to be of little concern to me.

It was then that the sentry cried. I froze. I couldn't see any shadow overhead and I hadn't seen any coyote or bobcat lurking about. I assumed it was a false alarm and we'd soon get the all-clear signal. It didn't come. Instead the second alarm was sounded and I followed instinct and scurried for home.

I ducked in just as I had been taught. Father was there waiting at the entrance taking the family count in Mother's place.

"Where's Mother?" I asked breathlessly.

"She hasn't come yet," said Father with a worried look on his face.

"What is it?" I asked next.

"A stampede," said Father.

"Stampede?" I had never seen one before. I don't think that I had even heard of one before.

"Cattle," explained Father. "Running cattle."

"Running from what?"

"I don't know," said Father. "I'm not sure that they know. They just run. And they run over anything that is in their way."

"Where do they run to?" I asked.

"Who knows," said Father. "They just run until they stop. I don't think that they are going anywhere."

It all sounded pretty silly to me. I was about to make some remark about us stopping the cattle from running over our town when I remembered the cow that I had seen many, many weeks earlier. I wasn't sure just which one of us would be brave enough to issue our order. I was sure that it wouldn't be me.

The sound was getting much closer now. I was feeling a little bit panicky and I guess Father was too. I was about to ask for permission to go out searching for Mother. I knew instinctively that Father wouldn't have granted it. It was our rule that no one ever leave the safety of home to go looking for a family member. Each of us knew that if home could not be reached, we were to duck under some rock outcropping or in a hollow or under some sagebrush—any place where there was temporary safety and then come home when all was clear. For someone else to go out would just put two lives in danger.

Even so I was thinking of asking permission when there was the worst noise I have ever heard. Hundreds of trampling, traveling feet began to pound away at the prairie earth above our heads. Dust sifted down the tunnel and started me coughing. Father was coughing, too.

"We'd better get down," he said. "Mother won't come now."

I was scared. Suddenly all of those near-truths and half-truths and white lies and outright lies loomed largely before me. I felt the guilt gnaw heavily at me and it made me feel a little sick to my stomach.

"I'll be down in a minute," I promised Father. "I'd just like to wait for a few moments more."

Father nodded in understanding and then he went on down.

I waited there for what seemed an eternity, waiting for the thundering hoofs to pass over my head. They seemed to go on and on forever. I was safe enough where I crouched—but what about Mother? What had happened to her anyway? She was usually the first one home whenever an alarm was given. I knew that it was because she wanted to be there to check in each family member.

But this time she hadn't come and I was really worried. Would she ever get home again? Had she been trampled by the herd thundering its way over our town? Would I never be able to explain things to her—to ask her forgiveness?

Suddenly I started to sob. I don't really know why. I just knew that I felt terribly miserable—and terribly sorry. If only I had a chance to make it right.

The tears and the dust mingled together and streaked my face—but I didn't care. All I really thought about was the terrible mess that I was making of my life.

First of all, there was my selfishness. Then there was my curiosity that had nearly gotten me killed a couple of times. To try to hide my selfishness and my careless choices because of the curiosity, I had resorted to lying. Then I had been mean and spiteful with Sandy. Now I admitted that it had a good deal to do with what Sandy was turning out to be. A bitter enemy. Then to cover the mess I had gotten into, I had resorted to bare-faced, black lies. It seemed that I was just digging myself in deeper and deeper. Now I wasn't even sure that Pepe still wanted to be my friend. And even worse, I wasn't sure what had happened to Mother.

The whole thing made me cry even harder. I was really a mess! Really a mess!

I didn't hear Sue Mary slip up beside me.

"Flick," she said softly, nuzzling her nose against my cheek, "is something wrong?"

I just mumbled a reply and cried even harder.

"Flick, Mother will come home. I feel just sure. She's smart, Flick. She'll know where to hide."

I wanted to believe Sue Mary. With all of my heart, I wanted to believe her. I just wasn't sure that she was right. And even if—when—Mother did come home, I knew that I still had to make things right.

Gradually my sobs stopped. I began to mop up my face, wiping it on the fur of my paws.

"Is something else wrong?" asked Sue Mary in a gentle voice. She knew very well that there was. She just didn't know if I'd be willing to talk about it.

"Me," I sputtered. "Me. I'm all wrong."

Her pressure against my neck increased.

"You're not all wrong," she defended me. "You might have made some mistakes—," she added thoughtfully, "but nothing that you can't correct."

"You really think so. You really think that—."

"Of course," she said confidently. "All it will take is a few apologies."

It sounded so simple. I wasn't sure that it would be that simple, but I was so miserable that I was willing to try almost anything.

Up above us the herd had stopped pounding our world into dust but the dust still sifted down the passageway. I choked again.

"Now, come down to the nest," coaxed Sue Mary. "You can't do anything by sitting here."

She was right. I followed her urging and went on down to join the rest of the family.

Chapter Fourteen

The Lesson

We returned to a different world after the stampede. Where there had been grass and vegetation, now there was dust and trampled mounds. It looked dismal and I guess we all felt a little sick at heart. The first worry for everyone was to find the family members who were missing. It seemed that Mother was not the only one who had not had time to get home.

The next worry would be our food supply. Oh, we all had a few emergency rations tucked away but we knew that they wouldn't last long. It would be some time before the prairie grasses would be able to grow enough to supply us. A few scattered, shattered stocks still remained, mingled with the dust, and a few roots were still there to be dug, but there certainly wasn't enough food for everyone. We all knew that.

But our first major concern was for Mother. As soon as the coast was clear, we set out to look for her.

I was busy searching for her, so intent on what I

was doing that I didn't even notice Sandy approaching me. I would have been nervous if I had, I guess, but then I wasn't thinking too much about myself just then.

Suddenly Sandy was standing right there before me. He had a smug, challenging look on his face and I knew that if I made the wrong move I'd be in trouble. And then I noticed something else. Sandy looked sad, too. I mean, in spite of his brashness, he looked just plain sad.

I was the first one to speak.

"Hi, Sandy," I said.

It wasn't much of a beginning but it was a start.

"Hi," returned Sandy, a little flustered by my simple greeting.

"I'm looking for my mother," I went on. "You haven't seen her, have you?"

"Your mother? Something wrong?"

He honestly sounded concerned.

"Yeah," I answered and I knew that the fear showed in my shaky voice. "She didn't come home before the stampede."

I couldn't believe it, but there was actually sympathy in Sandy's eyes.

"You want me to—to help?" he asked, hesitantly.

I managed a smile of sorts. "I'd sure appreciate it," I told him. And then I added, with a flush to my cheeks and my head bowed in shame, "I'm sorry about the—the—misunderstanding." And then I figured that I should really go the whole way and clear the air of the whole thing. "It was my idea to—to—pick on you in tag. I admit it. And I'm sorry."

Sandy looked confused for a moment. I was sure that he never expected me to apologize. Then he looked embarrassed. He looked down and kicked at a tuft of prairie grass that had miraculously escaped the stampede.

"That's alright," he mumbled. "guess we both need to apologize."

That was as close as Sandy got to an apology. It was good enough for me. We shook hands, grinned at one another and then parted company so that we could cover more ground.

It sure did feel good not to need to check over my shoulder for the approach of Sandy as my enemy.

Now my thoughts returned totally to Mother.

I didn't find Mother. Father did. She had been hurt in the stampede and Father had to help her home. It was hard to imagine that Mother, who was so cautious, had been caught away from home. She did have an explanation, though she chided herself concerning it.

She had seen Annabelle feeding off to her left and hadn't noticed her when she went home to bed with Louisa. When the alarm sounded, Mother watched and waited for Annabelle. She had broken her own rule and she scolded herself over and over for doing so, but at the time her motherly concern had ruled over her instinct. The first thing she knew the cattle were upon her and she was caught by the many rushing feet.

The only safety that she had found was a slight indent at the base of some rocks. She had ducked in there and flattened herself as closely to the ground as she could. The cattle passed right over her, kicking up dust, dislodging the rock and sending debris flying in every direction.

By some miracle Mother had evaded the flying, sharp hooves, but rocks and sand and scattering

objects had struck her again and again. She lay there, frightened, choking and bombarded as the stampede passed.

When it finally was over she didn't even have the strength to get home. She was sure that some predator would find her before any of the family members would.

We were all so thankful that Father had found her. We all gathered around to try to do whatever we could for her comfort. There wasn't much that we could do except keep her warm and quiet and try to coax her to eat a bit.

The days passed slowly. She improved but it seemed to take such a long time.

In the meantime, town life was all in a stir. The elders knew that it would be a long time before the food supply was what was needed. Several plans were discussed but the final outcome was that a good portion of the town citizens would move on and establish a new town site. Those who remained behind would feed on reserve supplies and what could still be salvaged of the grasses and roots. They would carry on until the new grass had grown again. Scouts were sent out and the whole town held its collective breath until they returned.

I found myself hoping to be one of the moving families. I knew that I would have no choice. The elders would decide. Still, it would be wonderful to see another part of the world. I gazed at the far-off trees and the distant hills. Perhaps we would even need to travel *that* far. No one knew just how far-reaching the stampede had been.

When the scouts returned with news that there was plenty of grass a few miles to the west and the families were picked to go, we were not among them. I knew that part of the reason was the condition of Mother. She certainly was not able to travel.

I felt disappointment but I knew that the decision was the right one.

Much to my sorrow, Pepe's family was one that was chosen to make the move. It was felt that the experience of Mr. Fotterby as Chief Sentry would be invaluable to the group as they traveled the dangerous miles until they could get themselves established again.

Pepe came to say goodbye. It was a difficult time.

"I took your advice," I said shyly. "I told Sandy the truth and asked him to—to *forgive* me." I don't know why that word was so difficult to say.

"I know," said Pepe, "I'm glad."

We both were silent for a long time.

"I've been thinking," said Pepe, "with me moving away and all, maybe Sandy can be your new 'best friend.' "

I didn't want a new best friend. I wanted my old best friend, but I didn't say so. It would have only made it harder for both of us.

"I'll miss you Pepe," I said instead. "I wish you didn't have to go—or I wish that our family was going, too."

"Me, too," said Pepe, but his eyes left me and traveled to where Sue Mary was basking in the sun, idly plaiting Louisa's hair.

He looked back at me, his eyes filled with sadness and then he smiled, just as Pepe always did. "Maybe I'll be back someday," he said.

"Don't wait too long," I warned in a soft voice. I had looked at Sue Mary, too, and I knew that there were several other fellas my age who were looking

at her as well.

"I won't," promised Pepe. "Goodbye, Flick."

"Bye, Pepe." And then he left me and went over to say goodbye to Louisa and Sue Mary.

I went back down to check on Mother and to bring her up-to-date on the town news. She was always interested in what was going on.

"Pepe's family is moving," I told her.

"Pepe? I'm sorry to hear that. He was such a fine young fellow."

We were quiet for a few minutes.

"What will you do for a friend now, Flick?" Mother asked me.

"I dunno," I shrugged and then added, "Pepe suggested Sandy."

"Sandy?" Mother sounded surprised.

Then she continued, with a question.

"After the beating he gave you?"

It was the first that Mother had spoken of the beating since it had happened.

"That was—that was—." I lowered my head. I had been hoping for a chance to talk to Mother alone. There was so much that I wanted to say to her. And now it seemed that I finally had my opportunity.

"That was a beating that I deserved," I said quietly.

Mother's head came up but I hurried on.

"I was mean to Sandy—always. I talked the other fellas into picking on him in tag. Sandy—Sandy figured out that it was me and he got mad. I don't blame him."

"And the time that you hurt your nose? Was that a fight with Sandy, too?" asked Mother.

"No—," I said slowly. "That really was on a rock."

"On a rock?"

"I had found some specially good roots. I tried to get every last one and I pushed and shoved and fed in so close to the rock that I cut my nose on a jagged edge."

"Why didn't you tell me that?"

"I was afraid that I'd have to share," I admitted sheepishly.

"Oh, Flick," said Mother in a soft little voice.

"I know," I said. "I was selfish—and foolish—and—."

"A mother doesn't expect her child to be perfect," she said softly. "But a mother does want truth. Can you undertand that?"

I nodded.

"I let you down—and I'm sorry," I whispered. And then for some reason I felt that I just had to share the whole thing, get it all in the open and ask for Mother's forgiveness.

"Sandy did jump me," I blubbered, "but I had it coming. And he licked me. He licked me good and he would have hurt me worse, too, but Sue Mary came and she fought him but he was too big and strong for her and then Louisa came and she smacked him and he was scared of her. And then the girls brought me home—and—and—that's the truth."

"I know," said Mother.

"You know?"

"I've known for a long time. I got the story, piece by piece from Sandy and the girls."

"You knew I was lying?"

"I knew."

I cried some more. Mother reached out a comforting hand and rubbed it against the place where the jaw had been injured in the fight.

"Flick," she said softly, " I was far more concerned about the damage you were doing to yourself 'inside.' I knew that the outside would heal. But the inside? I knew that it would continue to fester and grow—unless you did something about it. I am so glad you told me—so very glad."

"I don't suppose you can ever believe me," I sobbed. "I don't suppose you can ever trust me again."

Mother smiled. A soft, delighted smile. "I believe you," she said simply. "I trust you one hundred percent," and looking at her I knew that she did. I had never felt better in my whole life.